Peter Coe is a painter, writer, lecturer and arts correspondent. He has been an architect and a art dealer, he lives and works in Somerset.

For my inspirational wife and family.

Peter Coe

A NASTY WAY TO DIE

AUSTIN MACAULEY PUBLISHERS
LONDON · CAMBRIDGE · NEW YORK · SHARJAH

Copyright © Peter Coe 2023

The right of Peter Coe to be identified as author of this work has been asserted by the author in accordance with sections 77 and 78 of the Copyright, Designs and Patents Act 1988.

All rights reserved. No part of this publication may be reproduced, stored in a retrieval system, or transmitted in any form or by any means, electronic, mechanical, photocopying, recording, or otherwise, without the prior permission of the publishers.

Any person who commits any unauthorised act in relation to this publication may be liable to criminal prosecution and civil claims for damages.

This is a work of fiction. Names, characters, businesses, places, events, locales and incidents are either the products of the author's imagination or used in a fictitious manner. Any resemblance to actual persons, living or dead, or actual events is purely coincidental.

A CIP catalogue record for this title is available from the British Library.

ISBN 9781035811298 (Paperback)
ISBN 9781035811304 (ePub e-book)

www.austinmacauley.com

First Published 2023
Austin Macauley Publishers Ltd®
1 Canada Square
Canary Wharf
London
E14 5AA

Prologue

The machine-gunner's aim was either good or lucky. He hit both men below the knees and they crashed to the ground writhing in pain.

The men in the two military jeeps patrolling the high Serra had been continuing their search for partisans for the third day. Three men in each jeep trained their eyes for any sign of movement but they had yet to see anything suspicious. Their negative reports at the end of each day had made them a laughing stock back at base. They had earned the derision of their commandant and they were desperate to succeed.

Towards the end of the afternoon of the third day, they saw two men with rifles further up the mountainside. That was enough for them - the jeeps careered over the rough terrain towards the two men. They called out for them to halt but the two took fright and clambered over the rocks as fast as they could. They couldn't outrun the jeeps or the machine gunner in the front one.

The patrol men treated them roughly and tied their arms behind their backs. They did nothing to stop the bleeding. The sergeant began to question them, demanding to know where the partisan group had its base. The men knew nothing. They didn't know anything about partisans they said—they were just out hunting rabbits.

The sergeant didn't believe them and started pistol whipping the first man. He knew nothing and had nothing to confess as he continued to cry out his innocence. The sergeant grew tired of the process. He stepped behind the young hunter, slipped the noose over his head and garrotted him.

He began again with the second man who had watched in horror at the brutal death of his friend. He also said he knew nothing about any partisans and whimpered for the vicious pistol whipping to end. It did—he was garrotted as well.

They left the men where they had fallen soaked in blood. They knew the vultures would do their work as they drove off in search again.

1

The land was still covered with clinging morning mist as Roger Harmer took his dogs for their early morning walk. He would take his usual route down the farm track, around the churchyard, around the village pond, then up the hill behind. From the top of the hill, he would see the surrounding countryside emerging from the mist.

He enjoyed this start to the day when he could collect his thoughts and, this particular morning, anticipate the Wednesday livestock market. He had sent some sheep for sale and expected to buy some lambs to bring on. He will have a good chat with his fellow farmer friends too; it will be an enjoyable day off the farm.

As he reached the pond, he was brought up sharply. There was a body floating a few metres from the edge.

'Bloody hell!'

For some moments, he was paralysed by the shock, then he shouted to himself:

'Bloody hell, I'd better try to get it out.'

Roger was a practical man, so he ran back to the farm to fetch a long-handled bale hook and lock up the dogs. Using the hook, he was able to bring the body to the edge of the pond. It was that of a big man and he needed to get help to lift it out. Fred Davies's cottage was the nearest. He ran to it.

'Fred, Fred—come quick, there is a body in the pond.'

'Don't bugger about Roger, it's too early for your jokes.' he shouted back from inside.

He opened the door.

'Christ Rog, you're as white as a sheet. Come in, sit down, I'll get you a Brandy.'

'No, Fred. No. We need to get down there, I'm not bloody joking, we need to lift him out. Looks dead to me but might not be. We might be able to save him.'

'O.K. Rog—let me get my boots, then I'll be right ready.'

They ran down to the pond and stepped in at the shallow edge. They stood each side of the man but it wasn't easy to get a grip as the body was heavy and the wet clothes were slippery but together they managed to drag him out onto the path.

They turned the body over, cleaned off some duck weed covering the face and then recognised the man as the reclusive newcomer who had been renting a small cottage for the last few months. They stared down at the dead man.

'What do we do now?' Fred asked

'I dunno really but I reckon it would be best if I stayed here to keep anyone else away. You run back and phone the police.'

'Yes—that will be best.'

'And bring something to cover the body when you come back.' He shouted after him.

Fred made the call and went back down to the pond. They sat down side by side on the bench close to the covered body-two sentinels for the dead.

'Bloody hell Fred, I've never been in a situation like this—it feels really weird. Spooky to be sitting here next to a dead man.'

'Never been anything like this in Yurleigh,' Fred said. 'It will be in the papers and even on the TV news an' all!'

'Bloody hell, will it?'

'I'm sure it will be Rog—local news at any rate.'

'If we don't shove off soon Fred, we might get caught on TV—don't want that.'

'What's keeping the police then? I phoned more than half an hour ago.'

Ten minutes later, Detective Sgt Julia Tremaine arrived from Yeoford in response to the call. She met Roger and Fred who were patiently waiting. She saw that both men were in their fifties and both had ruddy complexions-proper Somerset, she thought.

'Good morning gentlemen. Who found the body?' she asked as she peeled off the small tarpaulin.

'I did,' said Roger.

'When was that?'

'Must have been a bit before seven o'clock—yes, must have been about then.'

It could have been in the pond all night or maybe even longer, Tremaine realised.

'Where exactly was the body? '

He pointed, 'Over there by the bull rushes.'

'Have you touched anything?'

'Only his jacket to drag him out and we wiped some weed off his face, so we could see who t'was. We haven't touched nothing else.'

'Do you know who the man was?'

'Yes, we think so but we don't know his name.'

'Did you see anyone else around? Did you notice anything at all unusual?'

Roger said he hadn't noticed anyone or anything different from normal.

They thought she was a bit offhand but maybe that was how the police always were.

After all, they had done their best and what thanks had they got? If the man had fallen into the pond, they had got him out—what more could they have done? Maybe she thought they should have left him there and not touched him at all—but he might not have been dead and they couldn't have left him there to drown, could they? It would have been better if he hadn't died but that wasn't their fault, was it?'

She asked them what they knew about the man. They said no-one really knew him, nothing was known about him, he had never joined in anything going on in the village. He didn't seem to want to get to know anyone. We all thought that was a bit odd but then he wasn't doing anyone any harm just keeping himself to himself, so we all just let him be.

'From the one or two people he had ever spoken to he was thought to have been European-French or Spanish or something like that. Somewhere hot anyways.'

'Alright—thank you. We might want to talk to you both again. Would you wait over there please?'

They walked off.

'Bloody hell, more ordering about,' Roger said under his breath 'We did our best Fred, didn't we? I'm not used to this being told what to do an' all. Still, we better wait like what she says. Bossy though, in't she?'

Tremaine rang H.Q. to ask for the SOC team and sat down on a bench by the pond to wait for them. She could see that the place would have been in pitch darkness during the previous night. She knew that the sky had been overcast and that there hadn't been a moon.

There weren't any street lights in the village and the one light outside the pub was too far away to have illuminated the area around the pond. She thought that it was very unlikely that anyone would have noticed anything happening.

When the SOC team arrived, they took over the scene and began their procedures. Straightaway, they taped off the gateway to the pond and the path beyond that. Roger Harmer and Fred Davies continued to hang around in the background doing their best to look inconspicuous. They didn't want to miss the action and anyway someone else might want to question them. That's what she had told them, wasn't it?

Three or four other villagers had seen police cars arriving and had drifted over to the gate. They stood outside the tapes, looking expectantly towards the covered body.

The SOC officers searched through the dead man's clothes. They found nothing but a soggy packet of Camel cigarettes in a jacket pocket and a handkerchief and a lighter in his trouser pockets. They took fingerprints from his water-worn hands.

Some members of the team were measuring the shoe and boot indentations around the pond. They couldn't get proper footprints from the wood chip path but they could establish the different sizes of the marks. One of the SOC officers asked Roger and Fred to tread in trays of clay-like stuff.

'We need to have your footprints too please' he said, 'so as to be able to eliminate you both from our enquiries.'

Roger almost smiled.

'Do they really actually say that?'

The SOC officers didn't find any marks around the pond of a size that matched the shoes the dead man was wearing. They measured all of them and were sure as they could be that none of the indentations had been made by the dead man. So he hadn't walked around the pond. He hadn't fallen in when taking a stroll.

He might have been pushed or thrown in. They could see a cluster of indentations at the point where the path reached the pond. He could have been pushed or thrown from there but the marks were mixed and overlapping-too indistinct to provide useful evidence.

Two of the officers were dragging the area of the pond between the bull rushes and the cluster of marks at the edge. They found only a rusty tin bucket and a child's Wellington boot full of sludge.

The inspector in charge of the SOC team called for the mortuary van—the meat wagon—to take the body off to the Pathology Lab.

Tremaine couldn't do anything further at the pond. She would only get in the way of the SOC team. She asked the two locals where the man had lived and they pointed out a small cottage almost hidden by trees.

'Show the other officers where it is as well would you please—when they have finished here.'

She opened the gate and stepped on to the gravel path snaking up the grassed front garden in a serpentine curve. When she reached the cottage, she found the door unlocked. Inside, at first glance, nothing looked disturbed or out of place, nothing had been thrown around. She scanned the rooms, they were neat and tidy.

Two rooms on the ground floor with a kitchen built on at the back. She went upstairs-two rooms and a bathroom above the kitchen. She thought it would have been an idyllic place for a couple or a couple with a young family to have a get away from it all holiday. It was more suited to that than being a possible murder scene.

She stopped ruminating and put on her gloves and overshoes to begin making a search. She didn't see any identifying documents in the obvious places. No letters, bills, bank statements delivery notes, nothing. She continued to look but still didn't find anything significant. There were menu cards from the local Indian & Chinese takeaways and the Kebab house as well as a calendar pinned to a large cork board.

The calendar was blank. A piece by The Times wine correspondent was also pinned up. It was a month old. Two Portuguese wines which she had recommended as best buys had been highlighted. Anyone interested in wine might do that. Also on the corkboard were business cards from a local butcher and a green grocer. Three packets of Camel cigarettes sat on a shelf below the corkboard. Nothing remarkable in that collection.

A copy of The Times lay on the kitchen table. The crossword had been started but he hadn't got very far. I'm not surprised, she thought, I have rarely managed to finish one and I'm English. If the man was European, it was a pretty good effort to even have had a go. She noted that it was yesterday's paper-2

March 2011. There was a letting agency handbook from Cot-lets, Sherborne in a drawer. She made a note of the number. She would phone them later.

There were two shelves with books in Portuguese and in English. Some European guide books and two Michelin guides in Portuguese. One to France, the other to Spain. There was a Portuguese to English dictionary. Was he Portuguese then? It looked like it and might tally with the highlighted wines. After five minutes flicking through and shaking the books, she found a photo stuck inside the cover of a copy of Joyce's Ulysses in its English edition.

Not the easiest of books and why, if he was Portuguese would he not read it in translation? Maybe his English was unusually good? Or maybe it was just a deliberately odd choice, so that he would remember where he had put the photo? Maybe the photo was a valued keepsake he didn't want to lose? And the book would keep it pressed flat.

The photo showed four casually dressed men sitting around a table in what looked to be a restaurant. A menu was just visible but it was indecipherable. Who were they and where was the photo taken? Who was the fifth person who had taken the photo? The men appeared to be middle aged but it was difficult to tell that accurately.

Men's clothes and hair styles don't change enough to pin point an era, let alone the year. She reckoned though that they were in their late forties and she thought that one of the men in the photo was the one who had just been pulled out of the pond. If she was right that would put a different complexion on the photo.

Upstairs, she found another Portuguese book and some Portuguese made clothes in the wardrobe of the larger bedroom. The toiletries in the bathroom were all British made except for the Antiga Barberia after shave.

Having finished their work at the pond, the Somerset Constabulary SOC officers turned their attention to the cottage. They taped off the gate and garden and pinned a notice to the gate which stated that it was a crime scene and that it was forbidden to enter the area. They went through the whole place room by room, surface by surface but found only the finger prints of the dead man.

The footprints too were just those of the dead man. If anyone else had been there he or she must have been wearing gloves and overshoes or had taken off their shoes. If there had been any kind of struggle and furniture knocked over the killer had straightened everything out again. It all looked normal, perhaps even too normal.

There were the remains of papers and the burnt stub end of a cheque book in the fireplace. The burning had been complete and nothing identifiable remained. Had the killer made that fire? The place was absolutely void of forensic evidence.

'Nothing much here Sergeant. If his fingerprints aren't on file, we don't have much to go on. There is a straight line of disturbance through the grass down to the pond, so it looks likely that the man had been dragged down there. There are no signs of a struggle on that journey, so he was probably unconscious or already dead when he was taken to the pond. The P.M. might come up with something helpful.'

Down by the pond, the mortuary van had arrived. The corpse had been placed in a body bag which was zipped up and stretchered into the van. It had driven off and the few onlookers had dispersed, knowing nothing more than they did when they had arrived.

2

In Yeoford, Dr Bill Kyte, the pathologist conducting the P.M. found that the man had been in his late fifties or early sixties and in generally good health. His skin had that slight olive colouring which made him think that he might have been French, Italian or Spanish.

He had most of his own teeth, which were in better than average condition and the dental work was not British. His clothes were British apart from his socks and shirt which were brands he had never heard of. The Zorro lighter which had been in his pocket was also a brand Bill Kyte wasn't familiar with.

He didn't drown in the pond-there was no water in his lungs. He had been hit on the head and garrotted. He was dead before he was dumped into the pond. But he may not have been killed there-he had been dragged to the pond either unconscious or dead.

Mud and some grass were embedded in the joints of the heels of his shoes and inside the backs of them. The shoes were Senhor Prudencio which Bill Googled and found to be Portuguese. The bottom of his trousers were well muddied.

There was no skin tissue, blood or hair under his finger nails, so there did not appear to have been a struggle. The garrotting looked like an execution. He had seen similar deaths in gangland killings when he was a junior pathologist in London.

He calculated that the man had been dead nine to twelve hours. He phoned his findings through to Sgt Tremaine.

'Do you mind if I come over? I would like to have another look at him myself and I will bring over our photographer,' she said.

When she got to the Lab and she could see the man's face after it had been cleaned up, she was certain that he was one of the four in the photo. He looked older than he had looked in the photo but he was definitely recognisable. She asked the police photographer to take a new close-up of his face and to get copies to her at the station a.s.a.p.

'How did you know he had been garrotted, Bill?'

'There is nothing else Julia that makes this deep impression and cut into the neck,' he said, showing her the wound. 'It would have been a braided wire garrotte—much like a grocer's cheese cutter. It would have been excruciatingly painful until asphyxia.'

'God how awful-what a nasty way to die. I hope I don't ever see any more garrotted corpses. But thank you Bill, it was very useful seeing him cleaned up and hearing from you how he had been killed. We will also now have a good close-up mug shot which will give us something to go on.'

At Yeoford station, she discussed what she had found at the cottage and the details of her discussion with Bill Kyte with her immediate superior, Inspector Fred Curry. He listened attentively, sucked his teeth and then said:

'From what you have told me Julia, the evidence points to him having been Portuguese. The method of the killing looks foreign too. I haven't come across a garrotting in my twenty years of service. I think we are going to need some outside help on this one. We had better speak to the ACC.'

Having listened to their summary, the Assistant Chief Constable considered that the crime was out of the normal run for the Avon and Somerset Constabulary. EuroPol might have to be involved to make searches. He decided it would be best to call in the Met.

They could deal with EuroPol, Interpol and the what have you Pol, he thought—rather them than us with all that Euro regulated palaver, fill in form this and form that; triplicate this and triplicate that, they're welcome to it. ACC Wilkins wasn't known for ever having tried new things and he wasn't going to start now. He wanted things to run smoothly, nice and smoothly. He was due to retire at the end of the year and he didn't want any ructions.

'Tremaine can work with whoever the Met sends down; you carry on with your work here, Fred.'

The ACC knew that Fred Curry, ironically known in the station as Hot Stuff, just wasn't and that Sgt Tremaine would be the more suitable choice. She was intelligent, keen and competent; yes, definitely the better choice.

ACC Wilkins made the call.

It was put through to one of the duty officers who acknowledged and logged the request. He then considered what to do with it. After a few minutes, he had a bright idea which he wanted to put to the Deputy Assistant Commissioner. He rang upstairs and asked to see him.

Commander Sam Redwood was known to be on leave staying with his sister not many miles from the crime scene for some fly-fishing on the Dorset Frome. The duty officer found his mobile number in the Yard directory and telephoned. The number rang and rang. At that moment, Redwood was wading in midstream. He had left his phone in the dry in his tackle bag on the far bank.

Sod it-he would have to wade across to get it. When he did answer his phone, the duty officer told him what he knew from the Somerset police and said that the DAC knew he was on holiday but as he was close to the scene, would he mind checking in with the Somerset force, going to the crime scene to see what they might have found and to generally size up the incident and determine whether the Met should get involved.

'Damn, blast and sod it. Sod it all.' He muttered to himself. The Mayflies were hatching and the trout were rising nicely. The river was beautifully clear and he loved to be in that water as it gurgled and flowed through the delicately flowered Rununculus. He had had an idyllic few hours and now he would have to abandon a potentially fruitful session.

He regretted the loss of the day's fishing and the annoying interruption to his short holiday. The realisation that he would have to leave the tranquillity of the river threw him into a bad mood. He packed up his gear and muttered curses as he walked back to his car.

He put the postcode the duty officer had given him into the Sat Nav but he didn't like the main road route that came up. He picked up the O.S. map which he had been using to get to the fishing spots and looked for a more attractive route.

Yes-he would take the by-pass around Dorchester and the B road through Piddletrenthide towards Sherborne. Much more like it, he thought as he drove along. The views over the top were stunning as the expansive landscape was shown at its best in the sunshine.

Hardy country, he mused and congratulated himself on taking the better route. He skirted around Sherborne went through Charlton Horethorne and then through the narrowing lanes to the quiet Somerset village of Yurleigh. The drive had been enjoyable and he felt himself becoming less annoyed just residually grumpy by the time he reached Yurleigh. He should be able to fish again tomorrow and as the forecast was fine, all might not be lost.

Tremaine had driven back over to the village and he met her at the cottage gate. He was surprised. She looked young to be a sergeant. He reckoned she was around thirty. She was attractive and well dressed in a blue jacket and dark blue jeans. Tall, slim but not skinny, blond hair cut shoulder length, grey-green eyes, good bone structure and a refined face; no, she was more than just attractive.

She did nothing to accentuate it though-she wore minimal make-up, just a hint of green eye shadow and a near natural coloured lipstick. Maybe she thought her good looks interfered with the job, that they made her less likely to be taken seriously? It has been known.

On her part, Julia Tremaine appraised the newly arrived Commander. Redwood was tall and looked like he kept himself fit. He had what she would call an outdoor complexion. Maybe it was from all that fishing. His dark hair was well groomed, he had remarkably intense blue eyes and a strong chin.

He was dressed in an old Donegal tweed jacket with leather elbow patches and brown corduroy trousers—the outfit which he must wear for fishing. She knew from Yeoford HQ that he would be driving straight to Yurleigh from the Dorset river. Yes, she thought, handsome in an old fashioned sort of way.

Tremaine explained what had been done, who she had interviewed and what had been found so far. She said she thought the man had been Portuguese and that he had been killed and then shoved into the village pond. She explained that the pathologist had identified garrotting as the cause of death.

'Garrotting! Good God-that is most unusual, really most unusual!' Redwood exclaimed.

'The SOC team didn't find anything of significance either here or at the pond, sir.'

'They did though reckon that he had been dragged down to the pond.'

She pointed out the trace through the garden grass and the longer grass beyond.

'Right—let's go inside, Sergeant.'

'I have had a good look around the cottage, sir and the most interesting thing I have found is this photograph.'

She handed the photo to him and he studied it. The four men looked to be well-to-do and they certainly hadn't been starving themselves He put the photo down on the worktop.

'Hmmmm.'

She continued, 'Some of his clothes are Portuguese, sir, as are his shoes and so are several of the books and some after shave.'

'I would like to take a look around upstairs,' he said.

He knew there would be no point in going through the whole place again, he trusted that Tremaine and the SOC team had been thorough. He just wanted to have a look for himself.

The murdered man had used the larger of the two bedrooms, the one facing towards the church and pond. The iron window was small. It had a stone surround and a single mullion. The handle of the forged catch was curved in the traditional way and the closure tongue slotted into the stone mullion.

The floor was boarded and well-polished. A vintage Oriental rug covered the boards close to the bed. A pair of shoes and a pair of leather sandals were on the floor. Some clothes were thrown over a chair. An alarm clock, a torch, a water glass and a book were on the bedside table. He picked up the book.

'Yes—in Portuguese,' Tremaine said.

It was Dia do Chacal—Frederick Forsyth's acclaimed thriller.

'Interesting choice.' Redwood remarked.

His wardrobe revealed a selection of good quality clothes. Barbour outdoor gear and Bodum casual wear. A couple of suits which Redwood thought looked a bit spivvy, one ready made from Saccor Brothers and one tailor made by Vernaccio both with Lisbon addresses. There were no cleaner's tags. Nothing in any of the pockets.

Tremaine had checked all that too. There were two hats—Italian made and a Burberry scarf. There were four pairs of well-polished shoes—all Senhor Prudencio, which Redwood knew to be a good Portuguese brand and a pair of Timberland walking boots which had been wiped but still had a film of mud.

He went into the bathroom, clocked the after shave, opened it and sniffed.

'A bit too sweet and spicy for my liking. I don't think it would sell well here.' He read the label Ribeira do Porto. Antiga Barberia.

'Hmmm—never seen it before, he must have brought it with him.'

'Yes. It does look like you are right, Sergeant-he looks to have been Portuguese.'

They went back downstairs and Redwood looked around again. He noticed that there wasn't a land-line telephone but then it was unlikely that there would be one in a rental property.

'Mobile phone?' Redwood asked

Tremaine had said no phone had been found on the man, on the path or in the pond or on the way down to the pond.

'There is no land line phone in the house sir, so he must have had a mobile phone. It seems possible that it was taken by the killer.'

'There isn't a tablet or lap top in the cottage either sir. Nothing that would help us trace him.'

Redwood then said he would like to look around outside and down at the pond. They both walked down to the pond so that he could fix the full picture in his mind. She showed him where the farmer had found the body and where he had been pulled out.

'You said that the SOC team thought it was probable that he had been dragged down to the pond. And that the Pathologist confirmed this. He might have been dragged down here unconscious or was he already dead?'

Redwood said aloud but as if to himself:

'Was he killed here or killed up at the cottage—which is the more likely?'

'More likely at the cottage, I think. He might have made a noise down here as he was being garrotted and the killer would not have wanted that.'

'But if he was killed at the cottage, why drag him down here?'

'Maybe the killer was underlining a point, maybe he had a grudge and the soaking in the muddy pond was meant as an insult. Difficult to see any other reason for making that extra effort.' Redwood commented.

Then he spoke directly to Tremaine:

'It is an unusual crime and I think it was right for your ACC to call us. I will inform the Yard that we will take on the case-with your help, of course, Sergeant.'

They walked back up to the cottage where he had another good long look at the photo.

'So, this is really the best evidence we have,' he said.

'I'm going to take it up to the Met now. The technicians in the Photo Lab can play around with it. If you reckon that the dead man was ten years or so older than he was when this photo was taken, it would be ideal if the lab could manipulate the image to show them all that much older. We will have to see what they can do.'

The thought of having to go back to London and miss out on fishing altogether brought back his bad mood. Frowning, he sent a text to his sister letting her know that he had to go back to London and that he would collect his fishing gear and the clothes on his next visit. He apologised for disrupting her plans, which he knew involved a dinner with someone she thought he would like to meet—another one of her match-making efforts. Actually, he thought, I'm probably well out of that.

'Alright Sergeant, I will shoot off. Give me your mobile number, no better—key it into my phone, will you and put my number into yours.' He passed his iPhone to her. 'I will ring you if we discover anything and you ring me if you come up with anything more down here And keep at it—leave no stone unturned as they say.

I want the whole picture in every detail. Nothing is to be regarded as unimportant. Get your officers to put some serious leg work into finding any local sightings, anything at all about the man. They report to you and you report regularly to me. I shall ask your ACC to assign you to this case as a priority.' He drove off in what Tremaine knew was an expensive Mercedes.

'God—Mr Grump or what?' she muttered after his abrupt departure. 'What's got into him?'

3

Back at New Scotland Yard, he took the photo down to the Lab. There, amongst all the high tech equipment, he found Brian Knox, the chief technician.

'Hello Brian—can you make this come alive for us? We need to know as much as we can about these four men and where the photo was taken. May we also have enlargements of each of them individually? And would you be able to doctor the photos to show the men as they would look ten years older? We think that it may be crucial to have up-to-date images. And then have them sent up to me as soon as possible, please Brian?'

'Right, Commander.'

He gestured to a younger man working at a machine Redwood didn't recognise.

'Over here please, Mervyn.' Brian Knox translated Commander Redwood's request into the Techo language of enhancement resolution in his instructions to the younger man.

'And pronto please Mervyn.'

When the photos arrived in his office, inspection showed that the murdered man was definitely one of the four. Tremaine had already wired him the new photo of the murdered man taken in the Pathology Lab and Sam Redwood was able to compare it with the enhanced mug shot just produced in the Photo Lab.

Yes, without doubt it was the same man. Mervyn had done a brilliant job. He had expertly manipulated the photos to show the four men as they would have looked ten years on, as they would look now.

He switched on his desk light to carefully study the set of photos and think quietly.

The murdered man was sitting at a table with three other men. The identity of all of them was as yet unknown. So was the identity of the photographer. Was he a fifth member of the group or just a waiter asked to take the photo? Close up enlargement of the menu had shown it to be in Portuguese offering a range of traditional dishes and a small selection of Portuguese wines.

The menu was a standard blank that had been typed up. It didn't give the name of the restaurant and it wasn't dated. Not a lot of help there. A framed reproduction engraving of the Elevador de Santa Justa hung on the wall behind the men and on the flanking wall there was an engraving of the Torre de Belem. So it may be a restaurant in Lisbon, Portugal certainly. He thought.

He had the new photos wired over to Interpol in Lyon and the Policia Judicaria in Lisbon, requesting their help in identifying the murdered man and the location.

Within hours, the Policia Judicaria responded with the identity of the man- Juan Xavier de Santa Cruz. He had been a known mover in the shady world at the edges of international banking and crime. Their records showed that earlier in his life he was a member of PIDE, the secret police of the Salazar regime. That was all they had on file for him.

PIDE, the Policia Internacionale e de Defensa do Estado, was set up in 1933 at the beginning of Salazar's Estado Novo. Originally, it was an orthodox force operating in public view but it gradually evolved into a secret cadre which would concentrate on suppressing political opposition. During WW2, Italian and German advisors helped to model it more closely on Mussolini's OVRA Organazzione per la Vigilanza e la Represssione dell'Antifacismo, which had been established in 1927.

The German version, the Gestapo, which was formed six years later was an advanced and even more effective version. Hermann Goring had established the Gestapo in 1933 and it was this kind of secret police force that Salazar sought to establish in Portugal.

As PIDE had developed and had become increasingly active it had become feared throughout the country. A whole apparatus of secret police, informers and terror had been installed. PIDE officers had been responsible for some appalling atrocities over the thirty six years of Salazar's autocratic regime.

There were no specific crimes recorded against Santa Cruz but then pretty well everyone in PIDE had got a white wash report when Salazar had stepped down in 1968. That had been part of the deal. Interesting though that he had been in the secret police.

PIDE had encompassed a wide range of clandestine activities from spying to assassination. Maybe he had been some kind of spy and the police role had provided both access and cover? But that was years ago—what had he been doing since and why was he in England, in Somerset, now?

Redwood wanted to know more about his recent history. He telephoned through to the Policia Judicaria in Lisbon, told the officer who had answered who he was, why he had telephoned and asked to speak to whoever was in charge of the investigations there.

'That will be Chefe Superintendente da Costa. I will put you through sir.'

'Boa Noite Chefe da Costa; may I speak in English?'

'Sure—we all know English here Commander,' da Costa replied.

'Are you able to tell me Chefe what Santa Cruz did after PIDE was disbanded?'

'No not yet Commander—we are still working on it. We are following several trails but none are giving us strong leads. I will let you know what we come up with. Do you have a direct line on which I can reach you?'

Redwood gave him the number.

'Do you think his murder may be linked to his time in PIDE or that it would have had nothing to do with it? It isn't often that we have a murdered Portuguese man on our hands Chefe. And he was garrotted—virtually unheard of here. We need to find out if the crime originated here or whether someone had traced him from Lisbon and hunted him down in Somerset.'

'Commander—many PIDE men were pursued and killed by families who had suffered at their hands, so it is possible that it was the case here. But it is also possible that it wasn't. We are trying to keep an open mind at the moment. The fact that he was killed in England doesn't make it any easier for us, so we would appreciate receiving any information you think might be helpful to us.'

'We will certainly send you anything we find Chefe and I shall also wait for you to be in touch with whatever more you can tell us about Santa Cruz. So—for the moment Chefe, good hunting and goodbye.'

Chefe da Costa was baffled—he wasn't going hunting. Were all the English obsessed with chasing after foxes?

Da Costa turned to his Sargento Gloria Esteban.

'Gloria, get some of the boys to dig into what records they can find on PIDE operations in case Santa Cruz gets a mention. There just could be some mug shots on record but I fear that they will only come across a lot of deletions and dead ends. PIDE was very efficient at wiping the slate clean. But it should still be checked out.'

During their search, officers at the Policia Judicaria, locally known as the PJ, were able to identify a second man shown in the photos they had received from the Met. A Spanish fixer called Jorge Casals who had been brutally killed three months earlier in the mountainous area of the high Serra.

He had also been garrotted. The police in the town of Serta had responded to the general request for information sent out nation-wide from the PJ. They had wired through their notes, photos of the dead Casals and the PM report.

Da Costa phoned through to Redwood.

'Hello again, Commander. You will be interested to know that we have identified a second man in the photo. He is the one sitting on Santa Cruz's right; his name was Jorge Casals. He was killed in the mountains near here three months ago and he was also garrotted.'

'My word Chefe—there seems to have been a spate of garrotting, one over here and now one over with you; most alarming.'

'Yes—unusual here nowadays, Commander. PIDE men used to execute people in that way years ago, the hand-held garrotte was their trademark method but we haven't had a case since then.'

'Well, I hope you don't have any more, Chefe. Thank you for letting me know.'

He heard nothing further from the Lisbon police for several days.

4

At the PJ, they were in the middle of running the investigation into the death of Casals but still had not yet come up with any strong leads. They would now have to factor in Santa Cruz and would have to find out how the two men had known each other and whether their deaths were in any way linked.

The mode of killing suggested a connection but they didn't have any idea of the motive for the killing of either of them. If there was a link and two men in the photo had been killed by the same person, were the other two men in danger? Should they be warned? Who were they and how could they be reached?

On Redwood's instructions, Met officers telexed the information that had come through from the PJ down to Yeoford with instructions for Tremaine to bring herself up-to-date in case it could have some bearing on her enquiries in Somerset. She read and noted all that had come through.

She continued with her own thoughts and enquiries. Stones had to be turned that was what he had said.

She made the call to the letting agency. Cot-lets knew that the man wasn't local or even English. He had shown them an EU Portuguese Passport as identification. They told her that he had taken the lease on the cottage four months ago.

Tremaine realised that that was a month before Casals had been killed in Portugal. Had Santa Cruz known something that had caused him to get out of Portugal and come to England, Somerset?

Why had the men been meeting? Was the book significant? If it was, why in particular had it been chosen? Did the other men have copies? What would they use it for? Or maybe it was much simpler maybe, as she had thought earlier - the book was just somewhere Santa Cruz could place the photo and remember where it was? It begged a few questions though.

Was English the language used within the group of four men? Or were they all Portuguese? What was Santa Cruz doing in England anyway, in Somerset, in the middle of nowhere in Yurleigh? No-one visits quiet Yurleigh. Had he picked that village and that particular cottage to avoid something or someone?

An isolated cottage in the countryside might have been too obvious a choice. Had he considered it better to hide in plain sight, albeit in the sight of just a few people? A place where he could remain contained, quiet, private and un-noticed?

She had already noted that there had been three months between the two killings and that both men had been garrotted. If it was the same killer, did it take that long for him or her to find Santa Cruz in Somerset? Or was there less of a connection than the mode of killing would suggest?

Were they just two separate killings? She didn't think so—garrotting was not a common way to kill someone. It had pretty horrible undertones, it was a brutal emphatic death. It was meant to be. It was a very nasty way to die.

These were the sum of Sgt Tremaine's thoughts so far. Commander Redwood had asked her to report to him daily, so she made the phone call to the Yard. When, after a short delay she was put through, he could have been a different person, he sounded almost cheerful. They discussed the discoveries made by the Policia Judicaria in Lisbon. Two of the men were now known. She ran through her own thoughts about Santa Cruz.

He grunted an approval.

'Yes interesting Sergeant, good. Keep at it.'

Under the terms of the mutual crime-fighting arrangements, The Commandente of the Policia Judicaria contacted the Met and asked the AC if he would second Redwood to help them with their investigations on the spot.

'He would be working with Chefe Superintendente da Costa. Together, they would look for the connections between the four men and those between Santa Cruz and Casals in particular. One killed in Portugal the other in England.

Our officers are good Commissioner and Chefe da Costa is first class but if you are able to agree to our request, it would be most valuable to have the experience of one of your senior officers as well.'

The Assistant Commissioner phoned through to Redwood and asked him to come to his office.

'It looks like some time in the sun for you, Sam - lucky beggar.' He explained the request from Lisbon.

Redwood was a bit surprised but after a few moments, he thought that some time in Lisbon would make a welcome change and the case looked intriguing anyway. He agreed to go and the AC phoned the Commandente to let him know that Commander Redwood would be on his way.

When Redwood got back to his office, he telephoned Inspector Hayward whose section handled travel arrangements at the Yard.

'Hello Bill, would you please get one of your officers to book me on a flight to Lisbon tomorrow? I would prefer a morning flight and I don't mind how early it is. Would they also book me in to the hotel Solar del Castelo from tomorrow night for a week please?

It would be useful to have an open booking and an open return flight as I don't know how long I will be staying in Lisbon.'

He phoned Yeoford HQ and told the duty officer to let Sgt Tremaine know that he was heading down to Lisbon. He gave the officer the phone numbers for the Policia Judicaria and repeated his own mobile number. He made the officer repeat them back to him.

'Make very sure she gets them,' he ordered 'and ask her to keep me up-to-date with her findings in Somerset. Remind her I want daily reports preferably by telephone.'

When he got back to his house in Chelsea, he made a couple of phone calls giving notice to the greengrocer that he wouldn't need deliveries for a while and asked the newsagent to stop his delivery of The Times. He switched the gas boiler to stand-by and made sure all windows were bolted shut.

He switched on the two lights he would leave working to deter intruders even though he knew it to be a futile idea. Everyone does it though for a sense of comfort, he thought. He took a well-used suitcase out from the cupboard and considered what he needed to pack. He realised that he needed to know what the weather and temperature would be in Lisbon.

He Googled Lisbon weather and it came up with an average temperature of 22 degrees and a 10% chance of rain. That meant he should choose his summer clothes. He had no idea how long he might be in Lisbon but he packed enough for a week. He could use hotel laundry services if he ran out.

Having checked that they still fitted, he packed two lightweight suits that he had bought from Austin Reed a good few years ago, four long sleeved cotton shirts, one short sleeved shirt and two pairs of Chinos; one navy one khaki, two pairs of lighter weight summer shoes and his favourite Bamboo fibre socks.

He put the clothes and most of his shaving stuff, toothbrush, hair brush and so on into the suitcase. His passport, tickets, camera and sun glasses went into a small leather cabin bag. He had just started re-reading Karenina, so that went into the cabin bag too. He thought the book was quite long enough to last him for the trip. He expected he would be offered a newspaper to read on the flight. He might even select a Portuguese newspaper to see whether he understood any of it.

The next morning, he took a taxi to Heathrow Terminal One and the first TAP flight to Lisbon. Though it was a short two and a half hour flight, Redwood's rank allowed him to travel first class. The flight was comfortable and restful. There had been very little turbulence and the smoked Salmon blinis with a small bottle of Adega de Pegoes had been better than expected.

He was met at Portela airport by Chefe Superintendente Luis Gomes da Costa who greeted him warmly. He wasn't as Redwood imagined him from their telephone discussions. The undoubtedly experienced officer heading up the team in Lisbon seemed laid back and laconic.

Maybe that is how it was in Lisbon.? He was fiftyish, balding, short and rotund; he had the look of a jolly man who enjoyed his food. He was a smoker—the edges of his bushy dark moustache were stained ginger. His lightweight suit was cut to be worn casually.

'Welcome to Lisbon, Commander.'

They got into an unmarked black Mercedes. The corporal driver sped them through the busy traffic to Rua Gomes Freire. The multi storeyed headquarters of the Policia Judicaria was a bleak concrete building which looked as if it were made up from layers of giant dentures. He didn't much like the design of the new Met building but it was a lot better than this.

They took the lift to the fifth floor. Da Costa led him into a large room where his officers had gathered. He was introduced around. Most of the team of ten officers spoke English which was a relief, as he, like most Englishmen couldn't speak any Portuguese other than a handful of learned phrases. Da Costa introduced him to Sgt Esteban individually.

'Gloria is my special Sargento,' he said.

Redwood thought she looked curvaceously attractive. Maybe just a touch too emphatically?

She gave him a warm smile and said:

'He says that because he can often persuade me to go out to lunch. Luis likes to eat well. You will see.'

'Yes—we should go for some lunch now,' da Costa said, 'but we don't have much time today, so we shall just go around the corner for a Pizza, if you don't mind Commander.'

'That will be fine, thank you.'

As they walked to the pizzeria, Redwood said.

'Chefe, I'm sure that the last time I was here all the policemen wore guns but I see that none of you have them now.'

'We have them, Commander but we do not wear them unless there are disturbances or we are making an arrest. Some policemen on street duty wear them, as a reassurance to the public I believe.'

5

The team at the PJ needed to widen the enquiry into Santa Cruz and Casals and get more substantial information on their backgrounds. They needed to find out how the two men knew each other and whether they knew each other well. The photo suggested that they knew each other that perhaps they all knew each other but it could equally well have been a one-off occasion.

Da Costa and Sgt Esteban sent the DCs off to look in the records in all public departments. They were also to visit libraries, museums, hospitals, doctor's surgeries and dentists to check whether either or both of the men were recognised and, if so, get what information they could.

They were to go to Army headquarters again and double check on what records of PIDE they might still be able to find. As Commander Redwood was fond of saying—they were to leave no stones unturned.

After the fall of Salazar, many PIDE men went undercover in the Portuguese African colonies. Had the two men also disappeared from sight in Mozambique or Angola? Had they become embedded in the emerging African dictatorships? Many had become advisors, military trainers or enforcers. Portuguese mercenaries had been everywhere then and ex members of PIDE had been prominent amongst them.

Wherever they eventually ended up, the reason had been the same. They had left Portugal after the "Fall" to escape the witch hunts. They knew there would be plenty of people wanting to take revenge on the secret police. There were plenty who had experienced the atrocities-the torture and summary execution of loved ones.

With Salazar gone, their protective umbrella had disappeared. They had had to get out anywhere but preferably somewhere where Portuguese was spoken.

Some stayed on in the ex-colonies but most drifted back to Portugal after a few years when they thought it safe enough to do so. In twos and threes, they dribbled back home.

The telexed enquiries about the two men Gloria had sent from the PJ to the Portuguese Embassies in the African ex-colonies had drawn complete blanks.

There had been no record of them in their files. Both or either of the men could have spent time in one or other of the colonies but they hadn't been there openly.

There would be considerable difficulties in trying to pursue that line of enquiry further through the police departments in the new governments in the now independent countries. They didn't contact the embassies in the Indian, East Indian and South American ex-colonies as they believed they were too far away for many men to have considered bolting to them. They would leave this line of enquiry for the time being.

Santa Cruz didn't go to Africa and neither did Casals. They went to Spain. Though Santa Cruz had had the senior rank Casals was the dominant personality. He had an almost mesmeric hold over Santa Cruz. Casals was homosexual and he knew that Santa Cruz would come to recognise that he was too. Casals's control of the relationship was forceful and he intended it to fully develop.

When he suggested that they should go together to La Mancha, the area of central Spain where he had grown up and which he knew well, Santa Cruz had readily agreed. They would find somewhere remote and live together quietly for a year or two to see out any storms emanating from the newly democratic Portugal. They would keep their heads down and remain out of sight.

Casals still had some acquaintances in the area who knew nothing of his time in PIDE or why he had left La Mancha years ago. Through one of them, they found and bought a run-down farm near Torrijos. The old farmer and his wife had wanted to retire and their sons who didn't want to run the farm had moved to work in nearby Toledo.

The old couple had been unable to keep the farm in good shape. Santa Cruz and Casals bought it cheaply. The farmhouse was rainproof and dry but not much more than that. The house with its outbuildings was not visible from the main road; it was reached by a long dusty track. It was perfect for them; they just had to make it properly habitable.

The house needed a lot of attention. The plumbing and electrics were decades old.

Several of the windows had rotted. The staircase and a lot of the floorboards were badly worm eaten. But they knew all this; it was why the place had been cheap to buy. In order to save money, they began to renovate the buildings themselves.

They learnt on the job doing much of the general work bringing in trained men just to renew the electrics and plumbing. They found satisfaction in the good honest work and the better they became the more they enjoyed it. It took a long time but they were not in any special hurry.

They made a good job of the renovation of their buildings and on the strength of that they thought they could offer their services to others. They reckoned that they had become at least as good as some of the small builders in the area and their skilled men had agreed to join them when required for the specialist work.

Casals & Cruz was set up as a jobbing construction business. They began with some simple jobs for people nearby. They performed well, they were efficient, considerate and tidy so soon the scope of work broadened and they began to get some bigger jobs. They were able to take on larger scale renovations of houses and farm buildings.

As part of the preparation for construction work, they often had to clear out barns and other outbuildings. They filled skips with broken tiles corrugated iron and glass and burnt the wood-wormed timber in the yards. Apart from the discarded building materials, they found more interesting items that had been thrown out.

They quickly discovered that the old furniture and discarded carts, barrows and tools which were no longer wanted by their clients had become collectable. They took a stall at the monthly Flea Market in Toledo and also sold to the trade from their barns.

They found that they did just as well from selling the old gear and bric-a-brac as they had been doing from the construction work. It was also a lot less tiring and they didn't need to employ anyone. They could avoid the tedious form filling about employee's earnings. They could work entirely in cash and avoid tax returns. Who made tax returns in Spain anyway? They weren't aiming to.

They didn't have to work regular hours five days a week either, they worked when they wanted to and felt like it. They made regular buying trips going further north in Spain and over the border into France. They would take off for a week or more and call on farmers, factory owners and inn keepers to buy anything interesting that had become redundant or anything that they thought they could persuade the owner to sell.

Anything that they thought they could make a turn on. They would stay at farmhouses, Logis and small hotels in the provincial towns and villages. They came to know these lesser visited places well.

Over the border in France, they had found the Sud-Ouest and the region around Dax and Bayonne to be particularly fruitful. They sometimes bought stuff at the Flea in Bayonne if they reckoned they could make a profit on it in Toledo but mostly their buying was done in the smaller towns and villages like St Palais, Orthez, Peyrehorade and Castagnede.

They didn't go further into France, they didn't need to; there were plenty of calls to make in the region they had become familiar with. They knew where to go to get what they wanted. They found that the small farmers and inn keepers appreciated the cash transactions and had begun to put items aside for regular collection by the two buyers.

Similarly in Northern Spain, they did well in the smaller towns like Soria, Haro and Estella. They found the small hotels suited them best; they especially liked those with good but modestly priced restaurants. They had often made the buying trips into a bit of a holiday.

When they had bought enough, they would load up their large SEAT van with the chattels and drive back down to their farmhouse. There they had large enough barns to store everything and they had found that the longer they stored it, the higher the price they could charge. They weren't in a rush.

One day when they were looking for things to buy at the Flea Market in Zamora close to the Portuguese border, Casals took fright. He had noticed that one of the stall holders was staring at him with a look of half recognition. Was he searching his memory for just where and how he recognised him? Was he about to realise that he had come across Casals during his brutal PIDE days? It was un-nerving.

'Xavier, we must leave and leave now. I will tell you why when we get to the van. We should go away from here immediately and drive back to the farm.'

'But what about that donkey cart we bought, which is still at the farmhouse outside Soria—we should collect it first.'

'No, this is important—we can't bother about that, we will pick it up next time. We have the farmer's number and I will give him a call. He will keep it for us. If any of our other usual sources have stuff they have collected up, they have our mobile numbers and they will call us. It can all wait. It is vital that we get out now.'

They had had no idea that da Silva had kept track of them through his agents in Spain or that the stall holder was one of them. Da Silva had been their commandant in PIDE but they had not heard from him since leaving the force under a cloud and getting out of Portugal after Salazar's resignation.

The stall holder had indeed recognised Casals from PIDE days and from being arrested by him for Black Market trading. Casals had given him a brutal going over and he would not ever forget that cruel face. He knew that da Silva would reward him for passing information on the two men. He talked to the other traders and got the mobile numbers of the two buyers from a stall holder reserving stuff.

When they got back to the farm and had unloaded the van, they could see that it had been a very successful trip. They had got hold of a lot of things that they could sell on at a handsome profit. They were pleased with themselves. They went into the house, picked up a bottle of Tempranillo and some olives and went out onto the terrace to enjoy the evening sun.

It was then that Santa Cruz got a phone call from Tomas Lopes da Silva. It was a shock—a massive shock

In a peremptory tone, da Silva had said:

'I want you and Casals to come here to Lisbon and run my security operation. I will require you to make some trips as couriers and I will need you to recruit another two suitable couriers; one in The Netherlands and one in Germany. Your work will be secret, you will be under cover, you will answer only to me and you will be well paid, very well paid. You will not discuss this order with anyone.'

'We will need time to think about your request, sir.'

'You will not need time to think at all Santa Cruz, you will both come straightaway. I demand it. This isn't a request, it is an order. I will expect you within the week.'

6

Down in Somerset, Detective Sgt Tremaine continued with her local enquiries. She visited the letting agency in Sherborne and showed the recent photo of Santa Cruz to the staff in the Cot-lets office. They confirmed that the photo was that of the man who had rented the cottage at Yurleigh four months ago.

They knew little about him except that he was Portuguese and Santa Cruz wasn't the name he had used. He had signed himself Alfonso Garcia. That was the name on the Passport which he had shown them for I.D. They had known he was foreign anyway from the way he had spoken and the questions he had asked about ordinary everyday things. He had been well dressed, drove an expensive car and had looked wholly respectable.

So, Santa Cruz had been using an alias. Though it didn't surprise her, it was still useful information to have. There was one thing though which was surprising. The agency staff had remembered that Garcia had said that he knew exactly where the cottage was and that he did not need to be taken over to Yurleigh or to be shown around.

He had already decided he would rent it. He had paid six months rental in cash in advance. He had also agreed to pay future rental dues in six monthly tranches in cash as well.

The Cot-lets manager had phoned the owner of the cottage—a retired dentist now living out his years in the sun in his new villa in Santa Pola, Alicante. He had been more than happy with the cash deal and instructed Cot-Lets to go ahead.

They had given him the keys, explained where everything was and how the hot water and heating worked. They told him he would find additional information in the tenant's handbook and that he could phone them at any time during office hours if he needed to know anything else. At Cot-lets, they were well pleased, they couldn't remember ever having made an easier letting.

Tremaine wondered how he had known where the cottage was. Yurleigh was a small village reached by narrow lanes not many people knew it. She knew that at one stage the pub had a good reputation which drew people in but that had long gone. If you wanted to hide away without drawing attention to yourself it really might be a good choice. It was likely that he had done some careful research and some driving around.

He might have found out that it was a quiet village where people would respect privacy. It was off-the-beaten-track and untroubled by tourists. If someone had been looking for him, he would have had some job to trace Santa Cruz to Yurleigh But someone had found him and had done him in and it hadn't been a casual act. Someone had indeed gone to a lot of trouble.

She needed to build up a picture. Where would Santa Cruz have gone, what did he do, where had he shopped? She showed the new photograph around the local town of Wincanton. No-one in the supermarket recognised him but then they worked shifts so enquiring there was a bit hit and miss.

Someone on another shift might have seen him. Who knows? Staff in the well-known butcher's shop were able to offer some useful facts and opinions. They recognised him from the photos. Yes, Alfonso Garcia. He was a regular customer and they knew he was foreign not just from his accent but also from what he bought - veal, spicy sausages, local game and Keen's Cheddar.

Not many customers regularly asked for veal. He hadn't always shopped in person but when he did he always arrived soon after they opened at 7:00. At other times, he phoned in his order which they delivered to Yurleigh. He was always polite, stiffly polite. They had never seen anyone else at the cottage with him. The amounts of meat and cheese that he bought suggested to them that he did not entertain.

He was also recognised at the greengrocer—Charlie's Fresh & Fruity. There, he bought a modest amount of peppers, tomatoes, grapes, figs and melons mostly imported things that Charlie called the exotics. Sometimes, he called at the shop but more often he phoned in his order and they delivered it. They had never seen anyone else with him at the cottage either.

At the newsagent/tobacconist, the owner recognised him from the photo and told Tremaine that he called in to buy Camels and copies of The Times. He would buy two or three copies in a week. He had said that he liked to try the crossword, which was good for improving his English.

He was recognised at the Post Office where he had twice changed 2,000 Euros for Sterling. Graham, the Post Master, had noticed that he seemed to have a lot of high denomination Euro notes. Once he had changed 5,000 Euros, which had nearly cleaned them out.

He was also recognised at the Shell garage—both from the photo and the owner remembering his marked "continental" accent. The owner said he always put top grade fuel into his Audi.

'He fussed over his car—like a lover,' he said.

He had only been in the King's Head twice and only to buy bottles of cider to take back to the cottage. He wasn't a drinker of English beer and, seemingly, didn't want to mix with locals in the village.

She called on the churchwarden who told her that Santa Cruz had never attended the church. He would have been noticed as no more than a dozen people ever attended when the occasional services were held. But, he would be unlikely to have been an Anglican if he was Portuguese. More likely a Catholic if he went to church at all, the warden had said.

She went to the local Catholic Church in Wincanton. The Priest didn't recognise him from the photo, he hadn't ever been to Mass there. But the priest did remind her that there was a sizeable Portuguese community in and around Wincanton, many of whom attended his church and the organised social events.

Tremaine thanked him for that information and as she walked back to her car, she wondered whether Santa Cruz had chosen Yurleigh because it was close to that community. She made a mental note to find out whether he had joined in any of the social activities.

Her investigations were not yielding a lot—no breakthrough anyway-just background information. She phoned Redwood to bring him up–to-date.

'Look, it will take time, it always does,' he said, 'but your groundwork is essential in building up a picture Sergeant, we need as much information as we can get. Carry on.'

She wasn't pleased as it was beginning to look like a lot of leg work for minimal results. She wasn't getting in a mood, she was just a bit pissed off but she had to resign herself to continuing.

What about his car? Owned? Rented? She asked the local garage, Cory Motors, to pick up Santa Cruz's car and to see if they could work out how many miles he might have driven in the last six months and anything else it might reveal. Corys said they had not serviced the car themselves but they helpfully agreed to contact Audi main dealers to find out if any of them had records.

They phoned Tremaine to tell her that Audi Yeoford had serviced the car. Audis don't need frequent servicing but he had actually taken it to them so someone at the agency might be able to tell her something more. Her base was in Yeoford, so she decided to call at the Audi dealership first thing the next morning on her way to the station.

The Audi garage was on the edge of town in a large and purpose made building which looked vaguely high tech. She thought it was probably meant to convey the reliability of the brand. She couldn't quite remember the advertising campaign but it was something about Technik; yes, Vorsprung durch Technik that was it.

She didn't know what it meant but it sounded impressive and reassuring. Inside, there were rows of gleaming new cars. She blanched at the price tags and walked over to the service reception desk.

She told the receptionist who she was and what she needed to know. The girl brought up the records for the car.

'Yes,' she said 'the car belongs to Mr. Garcia, it has had one main service and also a couple of minor services. Would you like to speak to the service supervisor?'

'Yes, thank you that would be very helpful.' She followed the receptionist to a small office in the middle of the building overlooking the workshops.

She was expecting a tattooed brawny but he was a wiry mild-mannered man who told her that Mr Garcia's car was three years old and left hand drive. He remembered that Garcia had asked for check-overs prior to making a couple of European journeys a little while back. He had said they would be 3-4,000 mile trips and that he wanted to be sure the car was in best shape.

He had insisted that the tyres were checked for tread depth and had had two replaced. The supervisor said he seemed to be obsessed with keeping the car in top nick and had had it valeted whilst it was with them. He looked through the workshop records and gave her the exact dates on which the checks had been made. They might now have the dates after which the journeys would have been made. Perhaps they would be able to work out the journeys in detail. It was a good start anyway.

She thought about what she had learnt as she drove to the station in her old BMW. Once at her desk, she followed her intuition and Googled the road distance between Yurleigh and Lisbon. It was 1,510 miles which would make a 3,000 mile round trip and, adding-in some associated driving around 3-4,000 miles in total. That fitted. That fitted well. Maybe she was now getting somewhere.

If her hunch was right and he did drive at least twice to Lisbon, why did he do that?

Why did he not take a flight? Were passenger lists too easily accessible? Did he want to get there under the radar? Was he taking something that needed to be taken by car personally? Was he taking something that he didn't want to put through an airport baggage check? Was he driving to meet the others in the old photo or was it something else?

She asked her two DCs to check Channel Ferry bookings immediately after the dates of the service checks. Portsmouth was the nearest ferry port and she thought he would probably have gone from there over to France.

They checked with P&O and Brittany Ferries. Nothing at P&O but Brittany Ferries confirmed that a car of that make and registration had been booked over to France twice. Each time it had been two days after the dates of the service checks at Audi Yeoford.

She again phoned Redwood and gave him a detailed account of her visit to the Audi garage and the assumptions she had made.

'I am convinced sir that Santa Cruz had driven at least twice down to Lisbon. The distance fits with the round trips he described to the service supervisor. It also explains the ferry bookings.'

'Yes, yes, Sergeant; excellent work. Excellent. Very well done, very well done indeed.'

7

When she had finished work for the day, she decided she would look at her old maps of France, Spain and Portugal and explore her tentative ideas. Arriving back at her cottage, she said hello to her cat Tomboy who had started purring on sight. The purring got louder as she stroked him. She gave him some of his favourite Felix treats and he was in bliss.

Then she opened a bottle of Nero d'Avola and poured herself a glass. She took a container of the Ragu she had made two days earlier out from the freezer, so that it would thaw out. She began to review her thoughts about what Santa Cruz might have done on his journeys.

She reckoned that he would have stopped overnight each way on those long drives. She could see from the maps that the most obvious route would have been to take the motorways down through Western France and through Northwest Spain. That was what she thought earlier at the station and that was still what she thought.

She had asked her two Detective Constables to find out what they could about possible places where he might have stayed and to look first at hotels in smaller towns around the halfway point either side of the Franco Spanish border.

She reasoned that he would not have wanted to go far off route and would not have wanted the hassle of finding his way around cities. She had asked them to narrow the search by concentrating on hotels in smaller towns and villages that had private car parking.

She just had a hunch that he would have wanted his car to be secure.

She took an old Michelin Guide to France from her shelves and put it on the kitchen worktop. She made a green salad and a dressing with a good olive oil and just a touch of Balsamic and mustard. She put the Ragu into the oven, grated some Parmesan, put some Tagliatelle in a pan and switched on the kettle.

She poured another glass of the Nero d'Avola. She liked Italian reds particularly those from Puglia and Sicily and this one was especially full and tasty; very moreish. One critic had described the Nero as poor man's Amarone. Yes, maybe he was right she thought; anyway, it was a lot cheaper.

Then she looked at the maps in the Michelin guide. She didn't expect to strike gold, she was just idling really but she could see a whole cluster of hotels around the halfway point of the journey just north of the Spanish border. She did the same with a guide to Logis de France which she had also used a few years ago. There was a similar result. She cross-checked the locations with her more detailed road maps and what she had first thought was possible now seemed probable.

She felt more confident about her hunch and by the time she had had supper and some more wine, she felt absolutely certain. She felt pleased with herself too and was pleased that her work had been recognised over there in Lisbon. Tremaine was ambitious and success mattered to her.

Success had always mattered ever since she had been at secondary school and at university. She didn't regard herself as "driven" but her work rate had always been higher than average. It still was. She was never satisfied until she knew she had done the best that she could do.

At the station, the D.Cs spent the most part of two days on the telephone checking out hotels. It was hard stiff-neck work. Their ears were throbbing and they looked punch drunk from the continuous effort. They made phone calls to scores of hotels eliminating them in turn as they turned out not to meet the full requirements.

They made their calls in English when they could do so but Tremaine had chosen them for their holiday knowledge of basic French and Spanish so one way or another they managed to get the information they needed.

Ultimately, they traced Santa Cruz to a hotel in Castagnede just north of the Spanish border. Tremaine checked the maps. He would have taken the fast coastal Peage and then turned off for Dax at exit No. 11 off the N10. Castagnede was a small village off the beaten track about 30 Km from Dax. The only hotel La Belle Auberge was listed in the Michelin Guide as a quiet but comfortable small hotel with a starred restaurant.

That was interesting—was he a bit of a foodie? She rang the hotel and the receptionist confirmed that a Mr Garcia had stayed at the hotel twice. She asked her for the dates of those stays. Each time, they were one day after the ferry sailings.

She reported this to Redwood in Lisbon and again, he was appreciative and encouraging.

'Excellent Sergeant, very good work—we will get that checked out at this end. Send me anything more that you find and ask your DCs to carry on, they may find other places where he stopped. I will copy you in with anything we find here in Lisbon. We may be getting somewhere. Good bye for now, Sergeant.'

'Goodbye, sir'.

From the PJ, they wired over the enhanced photos to Police HQ in Dax. Officers drove over to Castagnede to show them to the staff at La Belle Auberge. A waiter who had worked at the hotel for many years confirmed that he recognised Santa Cruz and one, possibly two, other men from the photos. And he thought the man they knew to be Santa Cruz had stayed at the Auberge more than once.

This was checked with reception and, yes, Mr Garcia had stayed twice. Two others who seemed to be his friends also stayed on the second time. The three had registered as Alfonso Garcia, Koos van Dongen and Frans Muller—the names on the passports they had left to be copied at reception. The first time there were four of them; the three already mentioned and a Snr. Delgado.

The officers made notes. They interviewed the waiter again who told them that on the visit when the men were together they had had discussions, sometimes it seemed to him, quite heated discussions over dinner.

They had been speaking in English but his English was limited so he didn't catch what they had been talking about. The French officers relayed everything from their notes to Sgt Esteban in Lisbon.

Three days later, the Somerset Police telexed again to inform the Lisbon team that Santa Cruz had also been traced to a hotel in Haro, Northern Spain; five days after the stop in Castagnede. The hotel was the Valle de Oja; a modest three star place located just outside the town. They could see from the website and Google Maps that it was nothing special but it was decent, secluded and had its own car parking.

She phoned Redwood to discuss this latest intelligence with him.

'I think that five days would have been enough time for him to get down to Lisbon, do whatever he had to do there and drive back up to Haro, sir,' she said.

'I think I agree,' Redwood replied.

'We will send our notes and the photos to the Guardia Civil and ask them to look into it. Your contribution has been invaluable Sergeant.'

'Thank you, sir—we will keep at it this end.'

From the PJ, Sgt Esteban telexed the photos and the file notes to the Guardia Civil in Logrono.

When they received the photos and the request from the PJ, the Guardia officers drove over to Haro to show the photos to the staff. The ancient red haired woman in reception recognised Santa Cruz and one other. She was hesitant about a third but thought it was possible that a third man shown in the photos had also been there but he had looked a little different from then. She couldn't explain in what way.

She confirmed the date and they noted it down. She remembered that the three men had met up in the bar and had then moved on to the terrace. They had had two bottles of Rioja Blanco and had then taken a taxi into town. All three had stayed just the one night having registered as Alfonso Garcia, Koos van Dongen and Frans Muller.

Yes, as in the photos, they had been well dressed and the porter had reported that they all had expensive new cars. They had the registration numbers of the cars as recorded at reception—one Portuguese, one Dutch and one German. The Guardia Civil telexed the information to the PJ. They were able to pin point the three men the receptionist had identified.

Where had the fourth man been? Why had he not joined the others? Why had both the recent sightings been of three men and not all four seen in the photo? Where was the man who had been identified as Jorge Casals? Had he disappeared?

The enquiry was gathering pace in Lisbon. Da Costa, Esteban and their team of officers spoke rapidly to each other in Portuguese. It was faster and more efficient for them than using English all the time Da Costa summarised the discussions for Redwood and of course they included him by using English as much as possible.

But he felt a bit out on a limb and that he needed a colleague to help balance the numbers someone with whom he could discuss his own ideas. He had been impressed with the work the Somerset sergeant had done and, as she was already familiar with many aspects of the case, he thought she would be able to contribute well. If she would come down to Lisbon that was.

He phoned Tremaine and asked whether she would have any objection to being in Portugal for a while. If she was willing, he would ask the Assistant Chief Constable in Yeoford to second her to work on the investigation with the Lisbon team.

She was very much taken by surprise but after a few seconds she replied:

'Yes, do that sir. Lisbon has always sounded exotic and I would be really pleased to join the team.'

When he answered Redwood's call, the ACC agreed, in fact, he was encouraging saying that Sgt Tremaine was making waves, was increasingly impressive and that a stint of "foreign" duty would give her additional useful experience.

He phoned down and asked her to come to his office. He encouraged her to take the opportunity.

'Yes,' she said, 'yes sir, I would be happy to go.'

He told her who she should speak to in order to get the chits for reclaiming payments for foreign travel, hotels and other necessary expenses.

'You might get some welcome sunshine Sergeant, enjoy the posting. I'm sure it will be a very different experience.'

She tidied up her desk, dumped some files on a hapless colleague, asked the two D.C.s to keep at it and keep in touch with her in Lisbon and then drove back to her cottage in Sandford Magna. She checked what the weather might be in Lisbon and packed the larger of her two suitcases with summer clothes. She would need some "work" clothes and possibly something smarter for the evenings.

She packed two pairs of her Boden jeans and two linen jackets she had bought in a White Stuff sale. She also put in a dress just in case it might be needed and a lightweight navy sweater. She put in the small selection of make-up that she used, toothbrush, sun cream and enough underclothes for a week.

She put a hairbrush, lipstick, sun glasses, her new iPhone and her copy of Julian Barnes's essays on Art-Keeping an Eye Open—into her leather hold-all bag. She would have time to buy a travel guide at the airport. It would give her some basic information on Lisbon and Portugal.

She made arrangements for Tomboy to be looked after and fed by one of her friendly neighbours who had said that she was delighted to be able to do so and wished her a good trip and an interesting time in Portugal. She still had enough time to catch an afternoon train from Yeoford to Waterloo and then pick up the tube to Heathrow. Once on the train, she made a call and booked in for the night at the airport branch of Inter Lodge which was conveniently placed for Terminal One.

At Inter Lodge, she had a lone dinner in the restaurant. It was over-priced and not at all good. She wasn't surprised that there were not many people eating. The Lasagne was underpowered and had been re-heated. It wasn't nearly as tasty as those she made herself. The salad was limp and had too much cucumber. The dressing was heavy on the vinegar.

She had just one glass of wine which was on the fade because the bottle must have been open behind the bar for too long. It was ridiculously expensive. She didn't risk a desert. She was glad she wasn't paying. No point in complaining though, nothing would change if she did, she just wouldn't stay there again. Ever.

Afterwards back in her room, she tried to pull a few threads together. They wouldn't pull not yet. She decided to take a shower because she wouldn't have time in the morning. The shower room was small but spotless and the bedroom was clean too. She lay down on the bed, switched on the TV and did a bit of surfing around.

There was nothing attractive in the usual clutch of inane game shows or the football match. She set the alarm on her phone for 6:30, started to watch what she thought would be the least awful of the quiz shows and fell asleep in minutes.

8

Redwood met her at Portela airport as she emerged in the Arrivals Hall. She was wearing a blue linen suit in the expectation of it being warm in Lisbon. She smiled at Redwood who said:

'Good to see you, Sergeant.'

'Well sir, it is good to be here.'

They found a porter to take her cases to the waiting car and the corporal drove them both to the PJ Headquarters.

After she had been introduced to the team members, six men and four women officers and had been given a summary of where they were with the case, Chefe Superintendente da Costa announced that it was time for lunch. He, Redwood, Tremaine and da Costa's glamorous Sargento, Gloria Esteban were to have lunch together.

Lunch was a serious business with da Costa. He said lunch didn't have to be expensive, it just had to be good. They walked a couple of hundred yards from the PJ until they reached a narrow street where there were several restaurants. Da Costa stopped at one of the least showy and ushered them through the steam fogged door. He had booked. He was a regular and was greeted as a friend by the Patron Gulio Enriquez.

The room was plain and the people already eating looked like local business people. There wasn't a menu you ate what Gulio had prepared. On this day, he offered a large platter of cured meats & cheeses followed by Bacalhau with fine beans and batatas fritas. It was all delicious and the house wine - an Alentejano - was remarkably good.

Julia Tremaine thought it an amazing way to go about police business; it couldn't have been more different from the joylessness of a sandwich at her desk in Yeoford. She thought da Costa and Gloria were very easy going and that Redwood was alright but a bit stiff by comparison. Maybe she could loosen him up? It might be an enjoyable assignment.

She took particular note of Gloria as a woman would and she could see that her silk shirt and fitted jeans had been chosen to emphasise her curves. Had she chosen them to upstage her? She had a generous mouth coloured with dark red lipstick and she had strongly accentuated her eyes and eyelashes. Good for her, Julia thought. God we would never be able to present ourselves like that at Yeoford HQ.

The foursome spent two and a half hours over lunch and discussion of the case. They discussed not only the facts so far gathered but also got into free speculation about the who, the how and the why. Gloria was especially switched on to speculation.

'Her forte,' da Costa said.

'Of course,' Gloria chirped 'a woman's intuition is always useful.'

Redwood looked at Tremaine and smiled, 'yes, I have discovered that.'

She coloured slightly.

Da Costa was well pleased. He and Redwood seemed to be getting along well working together and now, he had two seriously attractive sergeants to look after. He could see men at other tables looking with interest even envy and he was enjoying it.

He thought the two women would work well together; they were very different from each other, so they would not be competing. Gloria was extravagantly outgoing-Julia seemed quieter, steadier and outwardly more serious. He noticed that she wore very little make-up in contrast to Gloria.

'Yes, they will be fine.' he thought. 'They will work very well together.'

As they didn't finish their lunch until late afternoon, they decided that there was little point in going back to the station. They fell in with da Costa's suggestion that they should review again what they knew and chew over more ideas.

The corporal drove them over to Brasiliera-the Art Nouveau cafe-bar that permitted its valued customers to smoke in defiance of E.U. regulations. The large single space with its splendid wall of shimmering gilded mirrors along one side and polished brass bar along the other was blue with cigar smoke. Da Costa ordered glasses of the bitter almond Aquardente Reserva and bicas-the strong coffees.

'Not just the wines but our brandies and other digestifs too - you must try them all.'

Gloria had preferred a brandy and a bica. The smoke from da Costa's Portuguese Suave brand cigarettes was unnoticeable in the general fug. The English found the experience literally eye-watering.

After more discussion, two glasses of Aquardente and a glass of Sagres beer to finish, they decided they had done enough for the day. Several possible pictures had formed in their minds and the two senior policemen thought that it would be good to let these settle overnight.

Tremaine began to feel a bit nervous, her suitcase was back at the PJ and no-one had mentioned a hotel. Redwood twigged.

'Oh I have booked you in,' he said.

He explained that he didn't like brash modern "luxury" hotels and preferred those with local flavour. He had chosen the Solar del Castelo; a converted eighteenth century mansion within the castle walls

'You will like it,' da Costa said to Julia 'It is one of our top hotels.'

Their official car, a large black SUV was sitting beside a prominent NO PARKING sign. The corporal extinguished his cigarette and saluted. They were driven back to the PJ where Tremaine collected the suitcase and hold-all, then she and Redwood were driven to the hotel where a porter took her case into the lobby.

It was probably the most sumptuous hotel she had ever entered.

It was an essay in underplayed luxury. The walls and floor were covered in a creamy white polished marble. In the middle of the court, there were palm trees and a magnificent spouting fountain. The sound of the water splash underlined the atmosphere of luxury. Low slung deep leather arm chairs were placed in the arcade around the court and a few guests were sitting in them.

She had seen chairs like that in a design magazine; they were designed by a famous German architect in the 1920s, she remembered. While they waited for a different porter to take Julia's case up to her room, Redwood whispered:

'Euro Dosh-it's not coming from our budget, don't worry. Enjoy it.'

'I'm sure I will, sir. It looks like you know your hotels!'

Neither of them felt they needed anything more to eat. Tremaine said she was quite tired from the travelling and wouldn't mind an early night. By accident or design, their rooms were both on the second floor. They walked up the wide marble stairs and arranged to meet for breakfast at 8:00 - early for Lisbon.

They bade each other goodnight and went into their rooms. In her elegant and comfortable room, Tremaine reflected on how different it was to the low budget places where she and her last boyfriend had stayed three years ago. There hadn't been much finesse on those trips. There hadn't been much finesse about anything with him.

9

Breakfast had been set out in the old ballroom. The English detectives considered the decor to be a bit frothy for the early morning. They could have done without all that Roccoco stuff-all those cherubs and angels cavorting about among billowing clouds and sun rays in the highly coloured heavenly scene that had been painted over the whole ceiling. And God knows how it would look if they had had hangovers, she thought. Too much. Too bright.

Julia Tremaine didn't do breakfast, two cups of the excellent coffee and a single croissant were going to be her lot.

Redwood took a good-sized plateful of cheeses and cured meats with some crusty bread, freshly squeezed orange juice and a coffee. When he went back to the buffet for a little more, Julia caved in and selected a glass of the fresh orange and a Pasteis de Nata.

Redwood said little, evidently he didn't like conversation at breakfast. When she tried to make conversation, he just grunted. Well damn it, I won't bother. She was left to her own thoughts. She was still surprised at herself, one moment in Sandford Magna, the next in Lisbon. It was all a bit unreal. But it was going to be fascinating.

Breakfast done, they took a taxi to the PJ. Da Costa hadn't yet arrived but Gloria set them up with another coffee and handed Julia the report that had come through from the Guardia Civil overnight.

So had the three out of the four or maybe five, who had been in Haro been meeting about what had also brought them together in Castagnede and Lisbon? What were the connections between them? They badly needed to find the links. It seemed that they were or had been involved in business together. Doing what? And why were Lisbon, Castagnede and Haro the chosen locations for them to meet? Did they meet others? Had they met at other places?

Once da Costa had arrived, the four of them sat together to review progress.

They were now in a quandary. Investigations had to continue in Lisbon but what to do about the sightings in Spain and France?

After some debate, it was agreed that da Costa, Esteban and the local team would continue in Lisbon and that Redwood and Tremaine would get a car and follow the route Santa Cruz would have used to get to Castagnede and then to Haro to find out all they could up there.

They would be in phone contact to update each other every day. Everyone had everyone else's mobile numbers. Tremaine had set her phone and Redwood's into roaming mode.

He asked one of the DCs to contact Hertz and order a Mercedes SL. They would be able to drop it off at any Hertz branch wherever they were at the end of their trip. He was used to driving one and though his own was a few years older, he thought it would be helpful to have a familiar car on unfamiliar roads. The shiningly clean new model was delivered to the hotel. It looked the business.

They agreed that they would set out early the next day and by 7:30, they had had breakfast and were ready to check out.

Over breakfast, Redwood had said:

'I have been thinking, it might be easiest to do Santa Cruz's route the reverse way around and go to Haro first. What do you think?'

'Well, yes sir, it would be good to do that. It is a long enough drive to Haro. We can ask around there and when we have finished in Haro, it will be an easy drive up to Castagnede.'

They decided on it. Their route would be Lisbon, Coimbra, Guarda, Salamanca, Valladolid, Burgos and then Haro. A drive of about 850 miles but it would be on the new E.U. funded fast roads and the Mercedes was very fast.

'We will stop two or three times for coffee and anything else we might want and, just on the off chance, we can check whether Santa Cruz stopped at the same places.'

'Yes, good idea sir.'

At the desk, Redwood mentioned that they would like to keep the rooms as they expected to return to Lisbon after a few days. They had left most of their clothes in the wardrobes and had packed their smaller bags. The desk clerk said that would not be a problem to keep the rooms and that the hotel would be delighted to welcome them back.

He said: 'If I'm not mistaken sir, I think that you are both working with the Policia Judicaria. We are pleased to offer you a special rate.'

Santa Cruz wasn't recognised by anyone at their stop-off points but they had known it was a long shot even to ask. They changed over at each stop off and though Redwood did not usually like being driven he found that Tremaine was a confident driver and that he could relax. She absolutely loved the car relishing its power and speed.

They did drive fast, very fast reckoning that if they were pulled over their warrant cards and a bit of spiel about their mission would see them through. At worst, they would contact da Costa and get him to sort it out..

The hotel Valle de Oja was just off the road to Gasteiz half a mile out of Haro. The car park was shaded by tall Poplars. They parked between two of them and walked over to the hotel.

Having introduced themselves, they showed the photos to the receptionist with the fiercely coloured red hair.

'Yes,' she said looking at the photos, 'as I told the Guardia officers, these are the three men who were here. Yes, I'm sure now that this one was here with the other two. This one had tattoos on his arms and I remember now he had a funny looking nose.

They had drinks on the terrace and then took a taxi into town. I don't know where they went but probably to a better restaurant than the one we have here. I shouldn't really have said that but everyone knows this one isn't highly rated. If it was my hotel, I would have made a better restaurant and encouraged the customers to spend their money here.'

'That is a shame, Madam. A lot of people might wish to eat out of town, business meetings in particular. It would be somewhere more private.' Redwood agreed.

'Aah well, we have to do the best we can. Can I help you with anything else?'

'Do you know if they met anyone else here Madam? Anyone else who had business with them?'

'No, I think there were just the three of them.'

Tremaine then said they would like to speak to the taxi driver to find out where the trio had gone. The red head looked up the taxi service telephone number and showed it to her.

'Madam, would you kindly make the call for us? The taxi manager might not understand what information we need, if I am only able to speak to him in English.'

Having been told what they needed to know, the receptionist made the call. The taxi manager said he would look in the diary and the record of bookings then contact the driver and ask him to telephone back to the hotel. The call came after a wait of about twenty minutes.

The driver said he had dropped the three men in the Plaza de la Paz, the main square and had pointed out to them the street running behind the square which contained a number of restaurants. They had thanked him and said they would go straight there.

The receptionist said that she couldn't remember anything else about the men or their visit that might be of interest to the police.

'They looked and behaved just as you would have expected business travellers to look and behave.'

'Thank you Madam, you have been very helpful. We are most grateful. Now, we shall ask around in town.'

Once outside, Redwood said:

'Right that was useful; now to go to our hotel.'

He drove back into Haro and to what he knew to be a better hotel. Cloistros de Los Augustinos had been made from the conversion of a C14th monastery. It was big enough to have some rooms available and they took two in the same section on the first floor overlooking the covered cloistered court. It was just as sumptuous as the Castelo in Lisbon.

There was evidence of its medieval foundation everywhere. The overall monastic ambience had been preserved and wherever new elements had been introduced, it had been done with real flair.

They needed to freshen up after the journey and agreed to meet in the court in three quarters of an hour. They went to their rooms, had a shower and put on different clothes. All the rooms and their bathrooms had been made by the joining together of two of the former monastic cells.

The rooms were vaulted and the stone arches had been picked out against Lime washed walls. The stone corbels were intricately carved. The floor was covered in ancient glazed ceramic tiles. It was a showpiece and Julia Tremaine was enthralled.

When they met in the lobby, she said:

'Amazing. It is just beautiful, what a place. How did you know about this hotel sir?'

'Well, I stayed here years ago with my wife as a matter of fact. We used it as our base for exploring the Rioja region. We knew and liked Rioja wines and friends had told us that the countryside and the hilltop villages were marvellous and that it was possible to visit many of the Bodegas to taste and buy the wines direct. It was our first trip together.'

As meals are taken late in Spain, they still had time to explore the restaurant area in the hope of finding where the three men had dined. After two blanks, they found that the men in the photos were recognised at El Rincon. Not surprising, the restaurant was well known for its regional dishes and its selection of Riojas.

The glass entrance door and the window to the side displayed the starred recommendations of Michelin. Hachette, American Express, Decanter and several other rating organisations.

The restaurant itself didn't open until nine but the bar was open for evening drinks. Redwood enquired and was told that a table in the restaurant could be made ready for them in thirty minutes. They thanked the maître and ordered drinks to be brought to one of the tables outside.

When the waiter brought their Camparis, they explained who they were and why they were in Haro They showed him the photos and asked if he knew if any of the staff had noticed anything about the men or what they had been talking about. After a few minutes, a young man approached them, explained that he was a part time waiter and that he was a student studying English and French at the local college.

He had served the three men on that evening and he picked up that they were speaking in English, albeit with different accents. They seemed to be talking about their business and money. At one point, he thought he had heard one of them complaining that he was owed money and that he wanted to have it soon. It was the one with tattooed arms.

He had looked a bit queer and menacing. The group had paid up individually, which always a bit annoying as it took time to work out who had had what and how much it had cost. They had left the restaurant quite early. He didn't know where they had gone afterwards.

'Do you remember if they met up with anyone else here?'

The waiter said that they didn't, it was just the three of them.

They thanked him. They had a little more information now, money was a focus and the men seemed to have some sort of mutual business interest or joint enterprise. It wasn't just a casual group of men on holiday together. And so far, it appeared they had not met anyone else but they would need to cast their net wider to be sure of that.

Their table was ready and they moved into the stone walled interior. They were placed next to a stunning exhibition piece. A Matador's Traje de Luces, suit of lights had been hung on the wall and subtly lit. The pink and yellow silk garments were covered in pearls and beads and elaborately embroidered in gold. It was the only decoration on the wall. Nothing else was needed. They felt privileged to be sitting next to it.

They were both ravenous having had just coffees and a sandwich on the road. The 38 Euro menu offered mouth-watering choice. The wine list offered a selection of wines from the best Bodegas of Rioja Alta.

'We'll do the 38, I think,' Redwood said.

They studied the menu and made their choices. The waiter came to take their order.

'Please. You first,' Redwood said.

'I would like the Goats cheese & wild funghi starter, the grilled Grouper stuffed with Pequillo peppers and then Tiramisu with hot chocolate sauce.'

Redwood ordered the Crab, Prawn, Scallop and Vodka starter, the Beef Loin with asparagus and PX sauce and finally the Lemon Sorbet with Cava.

'And a bottle of Muga Reserva 2018, please.'

The dinner was well paced. They had plenty of time to discuss the case and to find out a bit more about each other. The Muga was a good loosener. Tremaine lost some of the defensive reserve, which was part of her normal protection from unwanted attentions. She began to feel more at ease with Redwood and responded more easily to his enquiries about her background and interests.

On his part, Redwood was gradually easing into a more relaxed interest in the young woman with whom he found himself travelling. He had realised that he definitely enjoyed being with her and being seen with her. Yes, he really liked it.

He knew she was single from the profile Yeoford had sent up to the Met. She definitely interested him but he was careful to avoid bombarding her with questions.

He knew not to rush and to let whatever might develop, if it did, do so in its own time.

He saw that she was regarding him with an insouciant smile.

She ribbed him a little.

'Interesting your choices sir, they all include booze. Is that normally where you start when you are making a selection?'

'Please, can we drop the "sir" stuff whilst we are here? They don't go in for it at the PJ anyway and it makes us look a bit out of key. Anywhere formal, if you have to, you can call me Commander. I think even that sounds better than Sir but otherwise Sam will be fine, thank you.'

'Right and you will call me Julia.'

All the dishes were superb and they both agreed that the restaurant fully deserved its reputation.

Redwood sighed. 'There is no way we would get a meal as good as this for the price in England. God knows how visitors can afford to take holidays in Britain.'

To complete their meal, he ordered a bica together with a good-sized glass of Carlos I Solera Brandy. The evening was still warm, so they took the drinks outside to enjoy the late evening street scene.

People, even some children, were still parading about in their finery. They felt very mellow after their excellent dinner. They walked back through the streets to the hotel in a satisfied silence.

10

As agreed, they met for breakfast at 8:00. Redwood was already drinking coffee.

'You're early, Sir Sam.' she remarked.

'Well, I have had a good walk around town. The main square was still quiet. Only a tabacaria and a small cafe had opened up. A couple of street sweepers were at work but there was no one else around. It was wonderfully peaceful. Then I noticed a noise like a soft wind and saw dozens of storks flying low over the rooftops leaving and returning to their huge nests on chimneys, parapets and pinnacles, anywhere high.

Some nests appear to have been formed on purpose made metal constructions. Civic nests! I hadn't realised they were such large birds or that they were so primitive looking. It was a fascinating sight in the early morning. Well worth getting up for. Amazing really.' he said.

'My God Sam, you are getting positively conversational,' she said laughingly.

Over breakfast, he said:

'It begins to look like a definite group of four or maybe five.' Then some silence and as they were finishing, 'We can drive around the town before going off to Castagnede, so that you can see the storks - we have enough time. You absolutely must see the storks.'

It took them just over two and a half hours to do the 180 mile drive across the border to Castagnede. They didn't stop enroute and arrived at the Auberge in time for a late morning coffee. They chose to have Americanos on the terrace. The day was warming up well and it felt good to sit in the sun.

They could see that the small hotel would have offered the privacy that the men seemed to have desired. The gardens offered complete seclusion even the car parking area was hidden away. When they had finished their coffees, they began their enquiries.

They asked the receptionist to confirm again the dates that the group had stayed. She gave them both dates. She also confirmed that they did not appear to meet with anyone else.

They then asked to speak to all of the staff on duty. They wished to speak to them individually. In turn, they spoke to chambermaids, cooks and waiters. Tremaine spoke to them in passable French but soon found that Redwood spoke almost perfectly. Well, of course he would. They didn't learn anything useful and after an hour or so, he suggested that they should have a simple lunch.

It had really warmed up and they decided to eat on the terrace, where the tables had now been laid for lunch. A large umbrella provided shade for each table. Redwood ordered a croque-monsieur and a green salad. He would have what everyone thought was a French recipe but he had been told it had originated in Portugal. She chose a grilled Tuna salad.

They would have a large bottle of Volvic water. When he had taken their order, Redwood asked the waiter if they could speak to his older colleague, the one who had recognised these men, showing him the photos.

'He will be on duty this evening, sir.'

After their light lunch, they decided to speak to several staff who had newly come on duty. Again, nothing emerged until they spoke to the gardener who said that at the time he had been trimming the Box hedges around the car park. He had seen the three men taking boxes from two cars and putting them into the third car. They were flat metal boxes about this size he said making a box shape with his hands - about 50 cm long and 20cm deep, he reckoned.

He thought that there were twelve or more boxes. Once the transfers had been made, there had been a fair bit of hand shaking and then they had driven off separately. He said that the cars were large and expensive looking but he didn't know about the makes, he didn't know much about cars he had never owned one.

Sam and Julia decided to have another coffee and think about what they had learned. They chose to sit in the shade now under the vine covered pergola. Who uses boxes like that and where might they have come from? Banks? Security firms? That seemed the most likely.

She phoned her colleagues in Yeoford and asked them to check with local cash transfer security firms to find out whether they used similar boxes. Redwood phoned da Costa, brought him up to date and asked him to get one of the DCs to make a similar check locally in Lisbon.

Before they had finished a second cup of coffee, the replies came in. Yes, pretty standard, used internationally boxes of that kind for secure cash transfers. Known as Transit boxes, the commonest size was 32 x 52 x 16 cm. They were pleased with that result and were considering what to do next when da Costa phoned.

The Lisbon team had now found that Casals, the man killed near Lisbon, had also been a member of PIDE and that he had regularly met with two or three of the others shown in the photos. PIDE was a definite link but they were still looking at other possibilities. They were exploring as widely as they could.

After some chat on the phone, Redwood told da Costa that he and Tremaine would head straight back down to Lisbon that was where the most progress was being made and that it would be sensible to have a complete resume with the full team.

'Julia, I think we should go back down to Lisbon now. We have good information on the transfer of the Transit boxes and Luis is building up a picture down there. If we need to talk to the old waiter, we can come back again or get him on the telephone.'

'Can we make it in one go?' he asked

'Yes, why not.'

Their route would be south from Castagnede down to St Jean-Pied-de-Port over the Bosque de Irati and down the Valle del Arga to Pamplona. At Pamplona, they would leave the slow twisting mountain roads and pick up the N1 to Gastiez-Vittoria, Burgos, down to Valladolid and on down to Lisbon, the same way that they had driven up. After Pamplona, it would be fast but boring motorway driving.

After St Jean, they climbed up the hair pin bending roads to the Spanish border at Valcarlos. The landscape had changed again. There were long vistas over the mountains. At the peak near Orreaga, they stopped to stretch their legs and enjoy the far reaching views.

Julia suddenly pointed and said:

'Look over there, three vultures circling.'

The more their eyes became attuned, the more vultures they could see.

'And there that's an eagle.' It surely was and as they gazed, it wheeled closer and closer until it was overhead. It was a magnificent bird.

'Fabulous,' Sam said, 'so glad we stopped.'

Back in the car, Julia said:

'You know Sam, I would like to know more about Portugal in Salazar's time. We can ask Luis about it. He will only have been a boy but he might have found out a lot from his parents.'

'Yes, we should ask him,' Sam replied. 'It might even give us more insight into Santa Cruz and Casals. It might tell us why they were garrotted, ugh, what a horrible way to die.'

'Well Julia, garrotting was the method of public execution here in Portugal and I mean public execution. Just as crowds of jeering spectators were entertained by watching the condemned being hung back home, here they could watch people being garrotted.

The condemned were strapped into an iron chair which had an iron spike protruding from a head piece, can't call it a head rest. The steel band attached to the head piece was placed around the person's neck and gradually tightened until the spike pierced the base of the skull of the choking victim.'

'God, can you stop the car Sam, I want to be sick.'

After that, Julia fell asleep and Sam drove on down to Lisbon.

They checked in again at the Solar del Castelo and asked for their bags to be taken up to their rooms. It was getting late and they were tired, they just had an omelette and a couple of glasses of wine in the Brasserie which stayed open 24/7.

Redwood thought that it would be nice to prolong the evening but knew that after the long drive, Julia would want nothing more than a shower and a comfortable bed.

11

Resistance to the iron grip of Salazar's dictatorial regime had grown steadily over the years and by 1965, a loosely organised group, Partisans for Democracy had been formed. They were sabotaging military installations and mounting small scale attacks on police and military patrols.

They were more of a nuisance than a credible threat to the establishment. Although the attacks were not reported in the censured press, word had got around and the establishment didn't like that. It did not like to appear to be vulnerable or to be losing control in any way.

There would be two or three incidents each month but so far they hadn't caused much damage. The partisans wanted to avoid civilian casualties or lateral damage. That would be counter-productive. They needed the public to get on side and definitely not to be antagonistic towards them. They chose their attacks carefully.

Usually they were showy token attacks, a grenade thrown at a bank or a smoke bomb thrown into a government building, a railway track blown up. The result was what they had intended, the public began to notice these signs of opposition to Salazar's regime.

In the autumn of 1966, they had stepped up a gear and in the high Serra, a group of partisans had shot up a military patrol, killing one soldier and wounding three others.

It was a deliberately noticeable event which was intended to show that they had acquired the capacity to wound the authorities. The provincial governor demanded action. The insurrectionary activities were not to be tolerated. They had to be stopped immediately.

The area command ordered that the treacherous criminals should be hunted down and punished. Control must be rigidly reinforced across the whole country and no weaknesses would be allowed. Commandente da Silva grouped his men together and ordered that they should form three patrols which would use all their vehicles.

Each patrol would have two Jeeps one of which would have a mounted machine gun. He selected six men for each patrol and gave them their orders. The territory to be searched was divided up between the patrols and they were to scour the whole countryside around.

Two PIDE men - Lt. Santa Cruz and Sargento Casals with four soldiers formed Patrol 2. They were ordered to comb the mountainous region of the Serra's where a group of partisans had been reported and where they were believed to have made a base in one of the many caves.

The patrol headed north from the barracks in Serta, crossed the Rio Zezere at Barragam do Cabril and moved across country towards Pampilhosa da Serra. They used tracks and bye-ways hoping to catch sight of any small band of insurrectionaries that might just show themselves.

They knew that their Jeeps would cope with the rough terrain and that the mounted machine gun on the front Jeep would quickly extinguish any resistance. They were in a bullish mood. But through the long hot day in the mountains they just saw some elderly goatherds with their flocks and their fearless Serra da Estrella dogs but no sign of any criminal traitors as their commandant had called them.

On the second day, they drove south to the Serra Candeiros but with a similar disappointing result. They saw three women dressed in black each with a few cows. As they got nearer to Santarem, they encountered small holding farmers who were mostly elderly men going slowly about their own business tending their crops.

They didn't see anyone who looked to be a threat to the state. They crossed the mighty Tejo and circled back towards Serta. It had been another dud day.

They were not getting anywhere. They were failing to flush out their quarry. Their negative reports had angered the commandant who was impatient for something positive that he could relay to the provincial governor.

What made it worse was that one of the other patrols had caught two armed men who they had executed bringing the bodies back to the barracks for gruesome display. There was a lot of bragging about it in the canteen. The PIDE men were becoming nervous that they would be disciplined for their failures and that the commandant would make an example of them in front of everyone else.

By the third day, they had become desperate to score a success. They marched into wayside cafes and tavernas and pulled out people for questioning. They learned nothing from the sullen peasants who, they knew, resented them and would not willingly cooperate in any way. The day was getting hotter and their frustration was increasing.

Late in the afternoon up in the mountains of the Serra de Alvelos, they saw two men with rifles. That was good enough. They drove the jeeps rapidly towards them jolting over the rough ground and sending up a cloud of dust

When they saw the military jeeps, the two young men panicked and began to run. The patrol sergeant shouted for them to halt but they didn't stop. Even though they were adept at scrambling over the boulders and rocks, they could not escape the advancing jeeps. The machine-gunner opened fire. Both men were hit and fell to the ground.

The patrol men got down from the jeeps and handling their captives roughly made the young men kneel whilst they tied their hands behind their backs. They didn't bother to do anything about the serious bullet wounds—both remained in pain and bled steadily.

They were ready to begin their questioning. Casals said he would take care of it. When the captives said they were hunting for rabbits, he said he did not believe them. The younger man had African blood and Casals decided to start on him. He hit the man hard with his pistol. He hated these scum who had come from Africa to infiltrate and pollute his native Spain and were now here in Portugal.

He hit him again even harder. The young man stuck to his story, we are here for rabbits. Casals worked himself into a rage of hate and continued to pistol whip the African until his face was a bloody mess. The man was whimpering piteously but pity was not available.

Casals stopped his work for a rest and to smoke a cigarette. He liked the strong black tobacco of Ducados Negros. It concentrated the mind. He offered one to Santa Cruz who, as usual, declined.

'You don't need to buy those expensive imported cigarettes Xavier, if you don't like my Ducados there are other local ones. Try them.'

'No thanks, I will stick to my Camels.'

'Ah well, it is up to you, now I must get to work again.'

Casals had been thinking during his smoke. He had to make one of the men talk and give out the information they wanted. The cigarette had done the trick; he realised how he could make the older one talk. He had become bored with beating the coloured man.

He stubbed out his cigarette on the man's neck, pulled out his garrotte, stepped behind him, slipped the wire noose over his head and began to tighten it. It was not a pretty sight. It wasn't meant to be, it was meant to terrify the older one and Casals was a sadistic bastard anyway.

The younger man opened his bloody mouth in a silent scream, writhing and kicking as the wire bit into his neck until he died without confessing. There had never ever been anything to confess. Then Casals started shouting at the older one and began hitting him saying that he would get the same treatment if he didn't divulge the names of the men in the partisan group and where they had made their base.

The man had no idea about the partisans and had nothing to tell. He was pistol whipped in the same way until he pleaded for Casals to stop. He did stop, the man was of no use to him, no use at all, he had told him nothing. Casals stepped behind him, slipped the noose around his neck and garrotted him too.

'Garbage, useless garbage people,' Casals said spitting at the dead men on the dusty ground.

The patrol had got nowhere. They had just added to the growing number of atrocities. They left the dead men where they lay, got back in the jeeps and drove off in search again.

The next morning, the teenage son of a small holder taking the goats to new scrub pasture saw vultures circling a quarter of a mile away. He went over to the spot. Though the vultures had begun their work on the men's faces and had pecked out their eyes, he could still recognise them—they were his friends from the village, they were just seventeen and nineteen years old.

As they sensed that Salazar was losing his grip on the country and that the public mood was turning against the government, the partisans intensified their activities. Government offices, police stations and military outposts were attacked more fiercely. The explosions were stronger and louder, now everyone could see and hear the opposition.

In the spring of 1967, a second military patrol was machine gunned in a village near Fundao. Two soldiers had been killed and five were wounded. The provincial Governor demanded immediate action from the regional PIDE command. The partisans were to be hunted down and firm retaliatory measures were to be taken.

12

After their long drive, Redwood and Tremaine made a later start. They had agreed to meet for breakfast at 9:30 to give them time to get up slowly and give time for da Costa to arrive at the PJ.

By the time she arrived for breakfast, Redwood had been out for an hour and had walked around the castle ramparts and the cluster of alleys within them and then down along some of the narrow streets of the Alfama below.

He had found a good guide book in the hotel and had read that Alfama was a derivation from the Moorish al-hamma and that the district, originally the Moorish medina had over time become a neglected run-down area before it had revived in the nineteenth century into what it was today.

He had enjoyed the historic completeness of the streets and alleyways and the small specialised shops selling particular and sometimes peculiar things. One sold only tins of sardines. Tins of various sizes, brands and colours with strong retro logos were stacked in pyramids in the window.

The window surround in its strong ochre yellow and the signboard above were original. So were those at the millinery shop with its fine lace and old fashioned veils and hats. So were many more. The shop selling Saffron and Pimentos was coloured in a rich Indian red.

The one selling olive oils and pasta was painted a matching shade of green. The early morning fish market was in full swing along the Rua de Sao Pedro. Even at that time, the noise was intense with the stall holders shouting over each other to promote their catches of the day.

There had been colourful fish that he had never seen anywhere else before. The best thing about the whole area he realised was that it was still a fully working district not an artificial creation. It had real purpose and vitality.

When he got back to the hotel, he was ready for his normal decent breakfast and Tremaine for her croissant and coffee. He noticed that she seemed much more relaxed, maybe the long car journeys together and the stop-overs in decent hotels had melted what reserve there might have been.

He sensed that she was enjoying herself. Enjoying the police work and, he flattered himself, she seemed to enjoy being with him.

'You absolutely must see the streets down below, Julia. Marvellous. We will go there later on. We will see what the others might plan but, whatever, we will have a walk around and a drink there this evening.'

'Sounds good to me, sounds really interesting. Great that you are doing the preliminary leg work, Sam,' she replied.

At the PJ, da Costa and Sgt Esteban took the team through the growing collection of notes and photos pinned to the "case board" There was a photo of Santa Cruz and of Casals with an array of notes below each photo. There were arrows crossing back and forth where the detectives had found possible links between the men.

They needed to get more of a handle on Casals. The evidence notes showed that he had been seen several times in the Bairro Alto during the winter and that he was thought to have had an apartment there. If they could find the apartment and search, it they might get more intelligence on the two men.

They decided they would go over together and make their own enquires on the spot.

Da Costa called for the SUV and they were driven over to the handsome district which overlooks the city. He asked the corporal to park outside the Brasilliera and they would walk in from there. It was almost impossible to drive around in the narrow streets of Bairro Alto and anyway they wanted to speak to as many people as possible who might have seen Casals.

It wasn't going to be easy because Casals had been dead for three months so people's memories might well have faded. They enquired at several bars where allegedly he had been seen and at a couple of the restaurants which were just opening their shutters. No-one recognised Casals from the photos and no new useful information was emerging.

The day was getting hotter and the two Portuguese were getting a little despondent. Maybe it wasn't such a good idea after all, maybe the gap in time was just too long?

'We should stick at it, Luis,' Redwood said 'Someone must have seen him and known where he lived. Someone must remember. Let's give it another couple of hours, otherwise we will have to start on a whole new approach and we will have entirely wasted a day.'

They continued their door to door enquiries with each pair of detectives taking separate routes. Redwood went with Gloria Esteban and Tremaine went with da Costa; the Portuguese speakers asked the questions. It was a slow business. In each place, they had to show the photos and wait for any response. The process began to be depressing as no-one recognised any of the men.

But at a tabacaria, the proprietor said he did recognise Casals from the photos.

'He used to come in every day for a newspaper and cigarettes. He bought Ducados Negros. He hasn't been in for a while though,' he said.

He thought Casals lived nearby in Rua Luz Soriano and that he rented an apartment there. Once he had come into the shop with another person.

'Yes,' the tobacconist said, 'this one.' when Tremaine showed him the other photos. He had identified Santa Cruz. Da Costa phoned Gloria and reported that they had had success and that they should meet up now outside the tabacaria.

'It is the Tabacaria Alto in Rua da Rosa,' he said.

The four of them felt an uplift, they must be getting closer to the trail of the two men now. They needed to find Casals's apartment in Rua Luz Soriano and search it, really take it to pieces.

Looking around for the advertising signs of letting agencies, they found two. There was no reply on her first call but Gloria's second call was positive. A mobile number was listed on the Apartamentos Central signboard. The call was answered by a woman; when Gloria asked to speak to the proprietor, the woman said she was the proprietor-it was her agency.

Gloria told her she was a police officer and then asked the question. The woman answered that yes, they did look after an apartment in that street and yes, it was let to a Spanish gentleman. Yes, a Snr Casals that was right, that was his name. Sgt Esteban explained that Casals had been murdered and that they needed to search the apartment.

The proprietor of the agency said that she was currently in Setubal but that, after she had finished her business there, she could get back to Lisbon and meet them outside No. 24 at four o'clock.

That was agreed. Fine said da Costa that gives us time for lunch. He knew just where to go.

'But first,' he said, 'you must visit Tavanos. We will just have a drink there. It is the oldest restaurant in Lisbon from 1784. You will find it interesting. We won't eat there though, it is too expensive and a little touristy nowadays.'

It was certainly worth the look for its dark and quirky interior with racks of dust covered wine bottles and cobwebbed ceilings adding up to a faux spookiness. A bit like Dirty Dicks in Bishopsgate Redwood thought, a bit of theatre. Their glasses of Anselmo Mendes Vinho Verde were cool and refreshing, it was the real thing.

'Far better,' Redwood said 'than the stuff you send over to us. I would like to take some of this back with me.'

'Good, we can arrange that. Now, we must have our lunch,' da Costa said.

His intended destination was a couple of alleyways further on. Bota Alta, known for its authentic traditional dishes and short lunch time menu. The interior was striking with walls painted in strong contrasting colours that the English pair now realised was very much the local tradition. Marvellously daring colour combinations which were clashingly vibrant.

Again, they didn't make individual choices, da Costa asked Gustavo the chef-proprietor to bring them what he would recommend. The wine came first—a chilled bottle of Adega de Pegoes from the nearby Setubal region. With the wine, a selection of hard cheeses and olives.

'Para boa boca,' Gustavo said. Bonne bouches just to get the tastes going. Then Sardinbas Assadas, charcoal grilled sardines, one of Gustavo's specialities. Da Costa wished to order another bottle and Gloria suggested a bottle of Lagoalva Tejo.

'We want you to taste all our local wines,' he said to the English pair.

After the sardines, a Feijoada arrived. Gustavo said that the subtly spicy creamy mix of pork, ham and beans was made from a recipe given to him by his grandmother. It was perfect to feed four.

It was time to ask da Costa.

'Chefe, would you tell us please what you remember from Salazar's time?' Julia asked. 'We have read about the period but somehow it seems too remote and it is difficult to properly understand what it was like here in those days.'

'Well Julia, I was just ten when Salazar stepped down but even at that age I could sense the tightness, the oppressive atmosphere of his regime. It had been like that for years. I was able to ask my mother and grandmother about many aspects of life in those days but it was almost as if they were still fearful to talk about it.

Portugal was isolated or so it felt. The Press, Radio and TV broadcasts were strictly controlled. People were told what the government chose to tell them and it was difficult to get uncensored information from outside the country.

A few brave intellectuals and politicians questioned the state of affairs but they like anyone showing signs of opposition were hunted down by PIDE and thrown into jail. My own grandfather, a banned Trades Unionist died whilst he was in jail on a trumped up charge.

PIDE, the police, any of the arms of state were not accountable. It was a very hard time for anyone who crossed the government, you could be black-listed and denied opportunities to work. Families who had been denounced could suffer badly and even starve.

PIDE used many paid agents who were ordinary people to inform on neighbours and workmates if they were critical of the regime and the state of affairs. Often, people were afraid to speak outside the family and there could even be an informer within your own family. It was dangerous if you didn't toe the line.

Now it is the opposite. We are in an open democracy. Trades Unions regularly organise strikes and virtually any pressure group can cause complete chaos but this is the case almost everywhere. I read that it is the same in England.

Most things are better now but not everything, we have to take the rough with the smooth. Oh dear, I apologise for rambling on. We had better get over to the apartment or we shall be late.'

They left the table and da Costa asked Gustavo to put the lunch on his tab.

The letting agent was outside no. 54 when they got there. She was nervous about allowing them to look around a client's apartment. Gloria flashed her warrant card, told her of the urgent necessity for the search and charmed them in. As the agent opened the door, it pushed against a pile of mail. She picked most of it up, took it inside and placed it on the lobby table.

The apartment was on the top floor with views of the Tejo estuary when they weren't blocked by other buildings. A few sailing boats were moving around on the narrow slots of water that actually could be seen from the apartment. You couldn't really say it was an apartment with sea views but Apartamentos Central would probably have hyped it up as such.

Knowing that Casals would not have been in the apartment for three months, Gloria asked about rent payments. They explained to her that Casals had been killed some months back. The agent said that the rent was paid by Standing Order set up by Casals when he had taken the apartment over a year ago. She would have the exact date back in the office if they needed it. There had been no problems with payments and no complaints from Casals.

They would need at least an hour and a half, maybe two hours to make a thorough search and that they could be fully trusted if she wanted to do something other than stay guard in the apartment. She said that would be helpful as she had other business in the area. She said she would see them in an hour or two and went back down the stairs.

The whole place smelt stale. Gloria and Julia immediately opened all the windows.

The apartment had a living room/dining room/kitchen, all as one open space and a large bedroom, a small bedroom a shower room and a lobby. For some reason, the two women suggested that they would tackle the bedrooms and that the men should tackle the large living space.

It all looked regular and tidy. Everything seemed to be in its allotted place.

There were letters, bills, restaurant cuttings, etc. on the kitchen table. But the whole place had a film of dust and looked like hadn't been cleaned for some time. There were some dead flies on the window ledges and in the sinks and it had smelt of stale air. Of course it did. Casals hadn't been there for three months and no-one had opened a window until now.

There were more letters, credit card accounts and bank account details in a drawer used as a desk. Redwood pulled the drawer right out and found behind it a copy of the same photograph but with the names written in biro beside each of the other three men. Xavier Santa Cruz, de Vries DV and just the first name of the third-Otto.

The photo with the names written in was a real find and they felt they had made a significant advance. They also found a diary which showed entries of visits to places around Lisbon and to The Hague. So, as they had already reckoned from the name, de Vries was probably Dutch and possibly lived somewhere in or near The Hague.

From the diary entries, it was probable that Casals had visited him there. Two trips to Lisbon were recorded three and four months ago and two visits to The Hague three and four weeks ago. Though the place was dusty, they could see that Casals had been reasonably tidy. Rubbish had been collected up and placed in the bin below the sinks. Da Costa tipped the contents onto the worktop. Screwed up bits of paper, the corks from two bottles of wine, some beer bottle caps, dried out Orange peel, an empty packet of Ducados Negro, some Ducados butts and three Camel butts.

They knew that Casals smoked Ducados, so someone else had smoked the Camels. They knew from the search of Santa Cruz's cottage in Yurleigh that he had smoked them.

The two women came out from the bedrooms trying to suppress their giggles. They hadn't found anything significant in the bedrooms other than that they reckoned Casals had been homosexual from the type of clothes he wore and the homo-erotic magazine at the bedside.

'Maybe all four of them were gay and that is what linked them,' Gloria said, 'maybe it was some kind of gay brotherhood.'

The men said that they had found notes that suggested the third man de Vries lived in the Netherlands, probably in The Hague and that Casals may have visited him there.

'Yaaah. Plenty of funny stuff goes on in Holland,' Gloria offered 'all kinds of stuff especially in that area up by the station in Amsterdam. You want to have a look at that magazine, Julia and I found it very revealing.'

'Yes, revealing it certainly was,' Julia agreed, widening her eyes.

The two women agreed that the living area of the apartment still smelt stale and said it was more than a bit musty in the bedrooms as well. The clothes would definitely need an airing.

'Scutty, typical of a man living on his own,' Gloria averred. Julia laughed, Gloria was always forthright.

The Letting agent returned. They said they had finished for now but that they would need to contact her again to allow another team to make a more thorough search and take away the clothes and other objects. They could see that she was very disapproving of the dusty surfaces, dead flies and the lingering stale air but they told her to leave absolutely everything as it was for the forensic team to investigate.

They closed and locked all the windows again, thanked her for meeting them and allowing them into the apartment and asked her to ensure that it was kept locked until the police team contacted her. They left and walked back through the alleyways to Brasiliera where their black SUV was still parked beside the same NO PARKING sign.

Back at the PJ, Gloria sent images of de Vries to the Rijkspolitie H.Q. in The Hague asking them to check for what they might have on the man. Julia wrote up more notes on Casals and pinned them to the board. It was now 7:40. Da Costa had an evening social appointment and Gloria had started yawning, so they decided to call it a day.

13

Redwood and Tremaine took the official car back to the hotel. They had agreed that they would take a shower, change and meet back down in the lobby. Redwood was sitting down trying to get the gist of a local newspaper when she joined him. She had changed into a long black dress with a squared neck line. He hadn't seen her in a dress before and he realised that she looked stunningly elegant.

It was a fine evening and they headed for the heart of Alfama. They sat down outside the first attractive bar where the tables were still in the evening sun. It had been quite a long day and a hot one. Now, it was just pleasantly warm. They ordered glasses of cool Vinho Verde.

'Mmmm, nice and cold but not as good as it was at Tavanos,' Sam said, 'what do you think?'

'Yes but it is fine and it is refreshing and it didn't cost as much,' Julia replied.

'It is just nice sitting here in the evening sun Sam, we don't have to have a cracker of a wine every time.'

Drinking their wine, they noticed that a small restaurant across the street had opened and they saw a few obviously local folk going in. When they had finished their wines, they walked across to have a look at the menu placed outside AlfamaMar.

'Wow, this looks just the job Sam. I can taste the seafood just from reading the menu.'

'Well, Luis isn't here to tell us that there is somewhere better, so let's give it a try.'

They didn't want a heavy dinner and some seafood seemed just right. The interior was plain and business like. There were no photos of Fado singers or visiting "celebrities" on the walls, which they considered to be a definite plus. They were shown to a table for two. Behind a larger table, they saw an engraving of the Elevador de Santa Justa and on the adjoining wall, the image of the Torre de Belem.

The shock of recognition that they were in the restaurant in which the four men had been photographed was dramatic

When the Patron came over to greet them, Redwood showed him the photo. He was pleased to see that a customer had liked to photograph his restaurant. When Redwood told him who they were and about the investigation they were engaged on, he was taken aback.

He said that he did vaguely remember the men because two had been foreign and the ordering had been done by the two who were Portuguese.

A fifth man, a tall man had taken the photo.

'But I didn't pay them much attention after that I'm afraid. They were speaking in English though. I do remember that.'

'Thank you for your help,' Redwood replied 'now we know that they had been here in the Alfama several times. But enough of policing, we are here to enjoy your cooking. May we ask you what you would recommend?'

He suggested they might like the shellfish soup Acorda de Morisco, followed by a sharing platter of the fried fish and shellfish of the day.

That sounded perfect. He ordered a bottle of Alentejano Branco to get going.

The soup was amazingly tasty. Rich, smoky and spicy. Memorable. The platter was a large one with a generous selection of crab, giant prawns, mussels, clams, fried octopus and goujons of mullet and cod. It was a dish to eat slowly and mostly with fingers. They both enjoyed this unfettered eating and licking of juices from their fingers

'Don't often get to do this back home.' Redwood commented.

'No. And it makes it all the more yummy,' as she wiped the edge of her mouth 'Someone once called it oral sex.' then she blushed.

Redwood ordered another bottle of the Alentejano and they talked about their own lives.

Julia said her father was a doctor in the Devon village of South Tawton and her mother taught at the Grammar school in Okehampton, the nearby town. She taught French and Italian. Her mother - Julia's grandmother had been French but Julia said she had never spent enough time with her to learn the language properly herself.

Both her parents were still living and working in Devon. She was their only child and had been much loved but she knew they had been careful not to over indulge her. They went on holidays together to France and Italy and it was on those trips that she was allowed to sample and enjoy wines, a bit watered down and got to appreciate wholly different tastes in food.

She had been a self-contained and serious child and when she moved to the Grammar School at Okehampton, she began to enjoy the syllabus and the results of working hard. She did well in her A levels and afterwards at Bristol University where she had studied English and History of Art.

'That is enough about me. Now where did you start?' she asked him.

Redwood confessed to having had a cushy time. His father had been a partner in the city law firm of Crossley, Redwood and Wright and the family had always been well off.

'Yes, our house was large and comfortable. There was a large garden, which was my mother's domain. My father kept a well-stocked wine cellar. He was generous and instructive. I think that was one of the more useful aspects of my education.'

It was assumed that Sam Redwood would join the firm. He had been to Westminster School and then to Cambridge. Pembroke College had snapped him up for the years in which he studied for his Law degree.

'I enjoyed those years in Cambridge and I loved the amount of music that could be heard. Many of those student musicians are now famous and acclaimed world-wide. It was wonderful to have been immersed in it.'

She said she too had loved her university time. She had shared a flat in a cul de sac off Blackboy Hill with two other girls. She had done all the things that students did then. She had steered clear of drugs but not booze. She had developed a taste for the cask sherries in the cellar bars around The Corn Exchange.

The sherry was good and it was the cheapest and most effective drink in town. She and her friends went there often. On Sunday mornings, they would sometimes go to The Coronation Tap—a Cider pub in Clifton where would meet up for a brunch with other friends. She said that they had played quite hard but that she had managed to come out with a perfectly good degree.

'After that I decided to pause and take stock. I didn't want to drift into doing what my parents expected me to do; to go into teaching but I didn't have an alternative in mind. Together with one of the other girls, I kept the flat and I went to work in Waterstones bookshop.

I enjoyed that, I enjoyed helping people and that was the time when Waterstones employed young graduates to advise customers when they asked.

The "from our own staff" book notes were a well-known feature that customers liked. She had written a few.

I realised after that year that I was certain that I didn't want to be a teacher and that I wanted a more varied life. More or less on a whim, I jumped sideways and joined the police. And so, here I am.'

Once he had his degree, Sam said he decided not follow his elder brother into the family firm. He thought that rather than practising law, he would help to enforce it. He decided to join the Met. He was fast tracked through the ranks and although he didn't let on to Julia, he knew that at forty-two he was one of the youngest of the "new blood" Commanders.

He talked about his wife, her being hit and killed by a drunken driver whilst walking home from the tube station after just three years together. She had been four months pregnant at the time. His long period of mourning had drifted on into a state of being single as a normality.

'I don't think about it much anymore, I am just me.'

'How about you?'

Julia confessed to never having had a lasting relationship.

'I am probably too picky and maybe a bit challenging. Anyway, no-one really came up to scratch and I wasn't heart broken when they drifted off.'

Redwood wondered whether the boyfriends were allowed to get close; close enough to really know her.

Neither of them had felt the need to do much about their single states and they both said that they had ignored the urging of friends and their well-meant set-up dates. The dinner parties with the mystery guest, 'who we think might be just right for you.'

They had stubbornly ruled out online encounters. They had grown used to being single and had realised that it did have some advantages. They could do what they liked when they liked-they weren't accountable to anyone else. They could focus on their jobs and they got a lot of satisfaction from that.

They found they had a shared interest in cooking. They liked to cook properly. They both said it was rare to fall back on any kind of "ready meal" or carry out. They agreed that cooking was often relaxing and therapeutic because of the need to focus on it entirely and leave any other thoughts behind.

'I like cooking Indian best, especially on a rainy Sunday,' Redwood said.

'Once I get going, I normally make a batch and put some in the freezer. That way, I can make several different dishes and enjoy them over a week or so.'

'I always start from scratch and it takes ages, enjoyable ages. It is so easy to get the spices and other ingredients in London-there is a fabulous oriental grocery just around the corner, so I am spoilt really.'

'I could be lazier and eat out more but I don't like eating alone and I think taking a book along just makes it seem sadder. Sometimes, I meet work colleagues or other friends for the evening but not often.'

'I enjoy cooking Italian,' she said. 'It is quick, easy and inexpensive. I don't eat a lot of meat and that is also easy with Italian dishes.'

'As it could be with Indian,' he chipped in.

'I don't eat out because it is a pain. Some men seeing a woman eating on her own just won't accept that it isn't a signal for them to come on to them and I'm not very interested in "girl's outings" as an alternative.'

He said, 'When you are in London, I will take you to a really good Gujarati restaurant—delicious vegetarian dishes.'

'No, not in Brick Lane that was done over years ago. The Indian restaurants in west London are a much better choice now.'

'Yes Sam, I would like that.'

They found that their tastes in books more or less coincided. They had both read and re-read the great English classics. Without doubt, George Elliot and Jane Austen were the very best-they agreed. Julia had also read a lot of contemporary fiction particularly novels by her favoured trio—Faulkes, Barnes and Boyd.

Sam said he hadn't read any fiction since he gave up on the late efforts of Kingsley Amis. He now read books on Twentieth Century politics and military history. He highly rated those by Anthony Beevor, so well researched.

Their tastes in music were a little further apart. He said he listened solely to "Classical" music and especially to recordings of early operas. He said he first heard them performed in Cambridge. He had, he said, an embarrassingly large collection of CDs.

Julia said she only got on with the more percussive music of the Twentieth Century; Stravinsky, Prokofiev, Shostakovitch and more recently Modern Jazz. She was keen on exploring the Jazz scene.

She talked animatedly about some concerts or Gigs by visiting American and European musicians. She ribbed him a bit for his narrow experience just stopping short of suggesting he was a bit of a fogey as she remembered their difference in rank.

'You must try a breakout Sam—try Jazz. Why not come with me to a really good jazz club with several bands playing though the evening?'

'I think I would like that, Julia—under your guidance, of course.'

They both liked to keep reasonably fit but neither did gyms. Some pleasurable walking but no jogging and no sports either, walking suited them best. Sam said he used to play Squash but had better not now in case he had a heart attack.

'The last time I played with my doctor—just in case.' he joked.

Julia said she was interested in the idea of wild swimming but was a bit wimpy about actually trying it as the water would be so very cold.

'Maybe I should try it here—in a warmer river?'

'If we get time, should we both try it, maybe up in the mountains?'

Throughout the evening, he had been studying her. He appreciated how she wore her beauty quietly, almost dismissively. She allowed her features just to speak for themselves. She was definitely not into show. She wore no jewellery other than a gold band on the fourth finger of the wrong hand, the European hand.

Probably another defence mechanism, he thought. He saw that her eyes were always alert and conveyed a sort of insouciance one might expect of a sophisticated French woman. She must have got that from her Grandmother, he reckoned.

For a moment, he compared her with Gloria. Julia was definitely the more naturally attractive of the two and he was certain her flame would last the longer. But that was irrelevant - Julia was just beautiful and he was pleased to be with her.

The dinner had been especially good and almost ridiculously inexpensive, so they decided to have good brandies - the Carlos I Solera again followed by bicas.

When they left the restaurant, they walked towards the castle mound. Sam said that it was the area that he had explored early in the morning. He pointed out the sardine shop and the milliners and the deliberately low level of street lighting which was all in keeping and helped to create the distinct ambience.

Whilst he was pointing out these features and she was looking about her, Julia tripped on a loose cobble and turned her ankle. He grabbed her arm to stop her falling and continued to hold it to steady her all the way to the hotel. It was painful, so she didn't take in that much more about the charm of the streets of the Alfama.

At the hotel, he asked for their keys and he helped her hobble up the stairs to their floor. He took her to her room and as he let go of her arm, said how much he had enjoyed their evening together.

14

She appeared at breakfast with a visibly swollen ankle. After they had finished their breakfasts of choice, Redwood asked reception to call for a taxi. He asked the driver to stop at the first farmacia they came to so that he could get a crepe bandage.

When they got to the PJ, he gave it to Gloria who wrapped it tightly around Julia's ankle. The binding tightness made it feel a bit more comfortable. She insisted that Julia should sit down whenever she could and suggested that she should do so now.

'If you could sit next to Julia, Commander Sam I want to give you both some notes.'

Gloria was excited. A dossier had come through from the Rijkspolitie.

'This is fantastic stuff,' she said handing the print-out sheets to Redwood for them both to read.

The Rijkspolitie had confirmed the identity of de Vries. He did live in The Hague. He ran a small scaffolding firm and employed four men He was known to be a member of the far right group PVV - Partij voor de Vrigheld. He had been photographed at their anti-Islamist rallies and had also been caught on camera with two others raising a Nazi salute at the gates of Dachau and at the site of the Kemna camp near Dortmund.

He had also been photographed waving a particularly disgusting banner at one of their White-Supremacy/anti-Jewish rallies in Rotterdam. He had taken part in their deliberately organised attacks on coloured youths at football matches. In one of these brawls, he had put three Muslim youths into A&E. and one into intensive care.

He seemed to have surfaced wherever there had been any racially motivated trouble. He had done two spells in jail for GBH. Clearly, he was a nasty piece of work. He was someone the Rijkspolitie had kept in their sights.

But and here was the headliner, just two weeks earlier he had been killed whilst on his early morning jog in the local park. He had been bludgeoned to death. The police were treating it as a random killing. Nothing had been taken—it hadn't been robbery with violence.

The body had not been concealed it had been left where it had fallen. There were no clues to the identity of his killer. There had been no witnesses. No weapon had been found. The police were searching in the dark for a motive and the perpetrator.

When the Rijkspolitie searched his small canal-side house and the scaffolding yard adjoining, it they found that de Vries had not been a tidy man. It seemed that as he lived on his own he didn't have to impress himself, just didn't care about mess. There were used saucepans and plates near the sink and empty beer bottles, glasses and half-empty coffee cups on the worktop. There was an unfinished casserole growing mould.

A chequebook and a bank deposit card, both from BWD Bank were in a deep kitchen drawer on top of copies of several magazines about guns, knives and military gear. In amongst these were some PVV propaganda pamphlets. Copies of the freebie right wing tabloid Spits were on the kitchen table and in the table drawer. There was nothing else remarkable amongst the kitchen utensils and tinned food strewn around.

In amongst the Spits were more PVV propaganda pamphlets and some copies of Elsevier magazine and The Armourer. Underneath it all was a Transit box, which contained a stash of cocaine in a sealable plastic bag.

The Rijkspolitie had wired all their notes to Sgt Esteban at the PJ. The drugs evidence took them by surprise.

Da Costa spoke aloud to the whole team.

'Now, we have three out of the four but are we on the right track? This evidence of drugs in a Transit box found at de Vries' house is disturbing. Could it be a drugs trafficking operation? Could the Transit boxes have been filled with coke and not cash? I will phone through to Rijkspolitie H.Q, thank them for responding so quickly and ask if they have any further details.'

The mood in the room darkened. Had they lost the plot? Were they back at square one? Da Costa phoned through to the switchboard and asked for a call to the Rijkspolitie in The Hague. The room stayed quiet for him to make the call.

Gloria spoke to him in a low voice.

'Whilst you speak with the Rijkspolitie, I want to take Julia along to the farmacia because I think they will have something better for her ankle than the bandage. We will go now and be back as soon as possible.'

At the farmacia, they did find a better ankle support made in a flexible plastic.

Gloria said, 'Now let's have a coffee over there,' pointing to Cafe Negroni. 'It is a well-known cafe and they will have a clean "ladies"; I will put the support on for you.'

'Thank you Gloria. I could do with a coffee anyway.'

They sat outside in the sunshine. When they had ordered the coffees and a Pastels de Nata, Gloria suddenly asked.

'Is your love life good, Julia? Do you have a live-in boyfriend who really cares for you?'

Julia said she did not have right now and that for better or worse, her love life was temporarily parked.

'Well, even that is better than mine,' Gloria said 'Alfredo has been with me for four years and it is getting stale, really bad. He is so lazy and self-indulgent, I don't know why I go on with it. He just doesn't care enough and I am not getting any younger.

I'm thirty four, you know. If I want to have a family I had better get on with it. Something has to change. I would like to be settled I think but not with Alfredo; I have had enough playing, yes I think I would like to settle down.'

'I'm beginning to realise that too but it has got to be right,' Julia said.

Gloria continued 'I would really like to talk to you for longer about it Julia, you know a really good woman to woman session. I think I could talk to you for hours about it because you are sympathetic and would understand but I guess we had better get back to work now.

Let's see if we can fix a night out together, then we can talk for a long time over dinner. If I can persuade Alfredo to go out, I will cook a very special Catalan dish I learned from my Spanish aunt and we will have some good wines.'

Whist they had been out, the Lisbon SOC team sent though their report on Casal's apartment. The great majority of the finger prints were those of Casals but there were some that had been made by Santa Cruz.

If they had time to run the tests, they would be able to get DNA evidence from the cigarette butts as well but common sense told them that the majority of the butts, the Ducados were from cigarettes smoked by Casals who lived there and that the few Camels were smoked by Santa Cruz. There were no Transit boxes.

The SOC evidence notes were added to the case board.

When Gloria and Julia returned, the whole team thought it was time to have a brain-storming session in order to come up with possible ideas for what might have linked the four men. They had also asked their colleagues in Interpol to intensify the enquiry into the identity of the fourth man, Otto-the only one of the group in the photo who had not been found.

The session produced a range of questions and ideas. They took it in turns to write down bullet points on the board.

Gloria offered her points:

- Had the four men all been colleagues at one time?
- Had they been members of the same group in the past?
- What groups had they been known to belong to?
- Were they all Gay? Was that the link?
- Were they just friends eating out together?
- Who else had they met?

Da Costa followed.
- They knew that Santa Cruz and Casals had been PIDE men but might the others have also been members?
- Were they all members or had they been members, of the new Rightest groups?
- Why were Santa Cruz and Casals killed?

A second sergeant on the team, Sargent Viera continued:

- They knew about four men but were there others involved?
- If it was cash in the Transit boxes, what was it for?
- If it was cash, was it providing funds to these groups?
- Who were they passing the cash to?

Julia wrote:

- The Transit box transfers were so far the only known link that actually brought the men together.
- We think they were making cash transfers but what if was drugs?
- If it was coke in the Transit boxes, where was it headed?

- If it was coke in the boxes, how was that distributed and sold on?
- Were they part of a wider cartel?
- Was de Vries at the nub of an operation trafficking drugs from the Netherlands down to Spain and Portugal?

Redwood chipped in.
- Were the others working for him?
- Or was de Vries just running a sideshow of his own?
- They knew about three meetings-how many more might there have been?
- If it was a funding operation, where would the money have come from?
- And where was it going?

Da Costa stood up again.

- It is known that some powerful banking families in Spain and Portugal lean to the far right and want a return to strongly governed one-party states. Could they be involved? Could they be behind it all?
- Were they and like-minded businessmen the funders?
- Or was the money obtained by criminal activity of the more usual kind?

Gloria took over again.

- Was the money or part of it, for the four men themselves?
- The argument overheard in Haro would suggest that they had had a personal interest in being paid. Did they each have a stake?
- What other links could there be?

They were in for a long intensive session to discuss all these points and others which would come up. There would be no time to break for lunch. Da Costa asked Gloria to order sandwiches, 'you know the ones we like' and wine from the local Deli. At 2:30, they had a short break to eat these and to have a glass of wine and another coffee.

Julia immediately realised that the sandwiches were nothing like those she bought in Yeoford, which were bland assemblies of soggy stuff in triangles of soft bread. These that had been brought in from the Deli were exotic by comparison, full of meats and cheeses with heavenly flavours in rolls, which had just the right amount of crust.

For a change, they were sparing with the wine - an ordinary Tinto and finished the break with the quite decent coffee made in the station.

After the break, they continued to review the various propositions which had been written up on the board. The weight of opinion still was that the men were most likely to have been passing funds in hard currency to others.

They thought that the amount of Cocaine would need to be greater than that which ten or twelve Transit boxes could contain if it had been a professional drug operation. But, on the other hand, it could be that a drugs operation was in its infancy and was set to grow.

If the Transit boxes were driven to pre-selected locations, who was the collecting courier? What was the destination of the collected boxes?

Was it a single courier from that point down to Lisbon? Was it one of the three men already murdered or was it the fourth man or maybe the fifth man who had been behind the camera?

Who was killing them? The killings had to be linked, they could not be random; that would be nearly impossible. Were they looking for the fourth man or the fifth man again as the killer? Or was the killer outside the group altogether? If so why would he have wanted to knock them off? If he was inside the group, why would he have wanted to kill three of them?

They sent further notes and a renewed request for help to Interpol and to the French, Dutch and German police.

The session had been a long one and they felt tired at the end of it. Da Costa, Redwood, Gloria, Julia and two of the DCs went around the corner for a simple supper of Pizza and carafe wine.

It was decided that they would reconvene at 10:00 the next morning. The official car took Redwood and Tremaine back to the edge of the Alfama. From there, they walked again through the narrow streets to the Castelo. Tremaine didn't trip this time but her ankle hurt after the long day and Redwood gently took her arm again.

15

The whole investigating team assembled once more in the case room at the PJ, having had the night hours to mull over the ideas produced in the brain-storm session.

Most of the team still favoured the idea that the money was being used to fund the outlawed groups. But they needed to follow up the drug operation possibility as well and two DCs were detailed to investigate this and make enquiries in parallel with those of the main team.

They would start by contacting their snouts embedded in the drugs scene in Lisbon and Faro. They would be looking for evidence that a constant line of supply had been coming out of the Netherlands via the four couriers or that one had been set up by de Vries as a side line of his own.

The main part of the team would continue to concentrate on the premise that it was a funding operation and that there were boxes containing cash

The insurgent groups were known to be well funded. They thought it probable that the origins of the cash were likely to lie with the powerful banking families and industrialists. Those who were known to be aligned with the politics of the Right.

The Public Prosecutor's office had had files on the directors of some of the banks for years but had not brought proceedings against any of them. There was not enough hard evidence and those prosecutors who were in the pay of the bankers would ensure that there would never be enough evidence.

Now, the PJ team would side-step official procedures and look again for themselves. It would be very difficult to trace the money directly to the controllers of the banks; people like that just didn't do anything overtly. Nor were they likely to have been careless-they employed aides and a whole pyramid of staff to ensure that didn't happen.

In Portugal, the banking families had always operated covertly controlling affairs without being seen to do so. They were remote, aloof and untouchable and they intended to stay that way.

The families in charge of the Banca Sociedad Alto and Banca Caixas in Lisbon and Banca Escorial in Madrid were the most obvious candidates but would trying to trace funds back to them get anywhere? They had used go-betweens, the four men to distance themselves.

BWD bank in the Netherlands and Deutsch Bank Bremen had also been flagged up by Interpol as being associated with the increasingly troublesome parties of the Right in the Netherlands and Germany.

But if the directors of any of these banks discovered they were being put under scrutiny, they would slam the doors shut. That would blow the whole operation. It was probably better to leave them for now and concentrate further on the four men and the fifth person, who still remained a mystery.

The searches through public records had not produced further information on the time Santa Cruz and Casals were in PIDE. As expected, information of any kind on PIDE and its operations was minimal. Those operations were part of a dark period in Portugal's history that had been deliberately expunged.

There was still a lot of leg work that needed to be done. Da Costa and Esteban allotted a city district to each of the officers in the team. In each district, they were to make door to door and street by street enquiries. It would be hard grafting leg work over long days, knocking on doors, asking people who were about in the streets,

Asking in markets, asking parents at school collection times, asking in shops and bars. They asked around for three whole days but they didn't find much to help them.

One of the DC.s found that Santa Cruz had been a private patient of the Dental practice in Chiado. The practice manager gave him a copy of Santa Cruz's records but said he hadn't checked in for more than a year. Once back at the PJ, he had wired the records to the Pathology Lab in Yeoford.

Bill Kyte compared them with the record he had made and yes, they were identical. It wasn't any kind of significant breakthrough but it did give further confirmation that Santa Cruz was who they thought he was.

Casals was known at the central library. He had borrowed books on antiques and Byegones, not often but he was a registered reader. Again, this was just a useful confirmation of identity.

The leg work enquiries didn't reveal any sightings of Santa Cruz and Casals together nor did they reveal either of them being with anyone else. They didn't reveal any records or sightings of the other two men but that was only to be expected.

CCTV footage at Banca Caixas main branch showed Santa Cruz making a visit and a cash withdrawal. The cashier shown on camera confirmed that Santa Cruz had a current and a deposit account at the bank. There was nothing unusual in that but it was interesting that he had chosen Banca Caixas for his own accounts. Banca Caixas seemed to be cropping up quite often in one way or another.

In parallel to the other two enquiries, one of the officers was to collect up to date intelligence on the emerging and recently established anti-Islamist and anti-Semetic groups throughout Europe. They were looking for evidence that any of the four men had been involved in Pegida and the Soldiers of Odin.

The ex-Isis fighters returning to Europe had also set up their Jihadist groups and the maelstrom of hate sustained between the groups and counter groups was growing alarmingly. Both sides were being well funded.

There were plenty of people who wanted a return to the old order and plenty who wanted to disrupt and change it forever. Some who just wanted to pull down the whole edifice of western society. The enquiries revealed a widespread and overlapping web of groups promoting violence vitriol and hate.

The pair of DC.s investigating the drugs possibility got the required feedback from their snouts. It seems to have been a small scale and intermittent operation run by de Vries. From time to time he would pass Heroin and Cocaine bought in Holland to his contact in Lisbon. De Vries was always paid in cash and made a tidy profit whenever he chose to do so.

When they reported their findings to the team, the view was that the drug business was incidental and on too small a scale to be worth further consideration. It was unlikely to have been the reason for the killings.

After several days, nothing significantly new had emerged. Nothing further had come over from Somerset either. The hard graft hadn't really paid off and the mood in the team had taken a distinct dip.

Da Costa found it harder to get any of them interested in a decent lunch, which hit him just as hard as the lack of further progress in the investigation. They were in the doldrums needing a new impetus.

16

They were revitalised when the Bundespolizei and GSG 9 in Potsdam telexed to say that in response to the Interpol alerts, they had searched their files and had found who they thought was the fourth man the PJ was looking for. Otto Kummel. He lived in Dortmund. He was thought to live on his own and was generally believed to be an efficient jobsworth accountant leading an ordinary life.

But apparently, he had another side. He was known to be associated with the Siege Culture movement and a member of the Blood & Honour faction perpetrating anti-Islamist violence particularly against the Turkish immigrants settling in Germany. He was part of Blood and Honour's Blitz brigade and had been to their training camps where they had been taught how to make violence really count.

They were often armed with knuckle dusters and Oyster knives. The knives were just the job for making disabling stab wounds without them being deep enough to prove lethal. He had been cautioned by the police twice at anti-Semetic rallies but so far he had managed to stay out of gaol.

He had come to light when the neighbour on the same landing in the apartment block had complained about the smell. The concierge had been asked to investigate. He had used his master key, opened the door and was immediately confronted by a swarm of flies. On the floor of the living room, Kummel's body was being consumed. The maggots were having a fine feast.

The neighbour and the concierge were badly shocked. He slammed the door firmly shut and accepted gratefully his neighbour's offer of a brandy and a sit down. Neither of them were young and the shock had unsteadied them.

The Bundespolizei were called. When they arrived, the concierge gave them his key saying that he didn't want to go into the apartment again himself. A young constable opened the door and was sick on the spot and even the more experienced sergeant backed out quickly.

The forensic team will have to deal with this mess, he thought. When the scientific police arrived, they opened all the windows, put on their masks and went through their procedures. They didn't find any finger prints other than those of Kummel himself. Nowhere in the apartment was there any evidence of anyone else being there.

They found credit card statements, bank books for DB Bank Bremen, a few other personal notes, souvenir football programmes, parking tickets, car keys and a typed-out Route Planner from Dortmund to Castagnede in France.

They realised that this was likely to be the fourth man that the Policia Judiceria were looking for.

A meat wagon was ordered and the attendants somehow managed to wrap the body firmly enough to get it on to a stretcher. They decided to use the stairs rather than have to upright the stretcher in the lift when God knows what might have oozed out from the wrapping.

The city pathologist conducted the post-mortem on the badly decomposed body. It showed that he had been killed by a single blow to the head, probably from a heavy instrument like a claw hammer. It had not been left in the apartment.

Once the apartment had been fumigated, the Bundespolizei officers went back to make a more detailed search. The clues to his identity lay all around. He was certainly Otto Kummel and apparently, he did live alone. Their searches confirmed there were no signs of anyone else having been there recently.

They interviewed the neighbour and the concierge together. Both confirmed that Kummel had very much kept himself to himself. They had only seen one visitor and they had seen him several times. He had short blond hair and a blond moustache. In the summer when he was wearing a Tee shirt, they had noticed that his arms were tattooed.

It was a "middle class" apartment block with basement parking. The concierge took the officers down and pointed out Kummel's three year old VW Touareg. They unlocked the car. The interior was almost showroom clean, deliberately clean. They opened the boot; there was nothing unusual there weren't any empty Transit boxes anyway.

There were two ticket stubs for Ajax Amsterdam matches in the small flip up compartment beside the driver's seat. Apparently, Ajax had recently played Bayern Munich and Chelsea at home. Was he just interested in any Europa League match or was he a fan of the Ajax team and their attacking style? Amsterdam was just a two hour drive from Dortmund, it would be an easy journey in that car on the fast roads.

It also was evident that he had made the long journey down to Castagnede and it was assumed that had met two of the others there and had passed over boxes of cash. So, where did that cash come from and why did he drive all the way to the South of France to pass it over?

The German officers had wired their notes in full back to the PJ and they were posted up under the new photo of Hummel. There were now four photos on the case board. They were the individual up-dated photos produced by the Met together with the Post Mortem photos of Santa Cruz and Casals. The column of notes referring to de Vries and Hummel were still short by comparison with the other two.

They had their four men but was there still an unidentified fifth member of the group? They would continue to assume that the "photographer" was associated with the group in some way. They still had to establish for certain all the connections within the wider circle.

17

Just as Santa Cruz and Casals had known each other prior to the formation of the couriering group, de Vries and Kummel had also known each other. They had met by chance during a riot at a football match. Ajax Amsterdam were playing Borussia Dortmund in a Europa League game at the Westfalenstadion in Dortmund.

The game was going along normally with each team making attacks and good defences with neither team becoming dominant when, possibly out of frustration, two players had laid into one another. The referee was having none of it and red carded both of them.

One was an Ajax player, the other played for Dortmund so the fans of both sides were equally outraged and were up in arms hissing and booing and making their protests known as loudly as possible. All around the stadium, there were shouts of:

'Ref off, get off, off, off, off.'

Soon the noise was immense, it seemed as if everyone in the entire stadium had joined in the shouting. Some started throwing coins, beer cans and bottles. De Vries and Kummel found themselves side by side, throwing cans and shouting abuse. Soon, all hell broke loose. It was complete pandemonium.

They were laughing and enjoying the fracas; it was more fun than the slow-moving game. As well as bottles and cans, fire extinguishers and any other detachables were hurled onto the pitch. The referee was hit and collapsed. Immediately, a general brawl broke out.

After a few minutes of complete chaos, the marshals surrounded the referee and tried to escort him off the pitch amidst more booing, cat calls and shouts of derision. The referee was called by names he wouldn't even have heard of. Sirens were heard, the police arrived.

Some went to the aid of the referee and the rest began to break up the crowd. But it was dispersing anyway with just a few pockets of active aggro left for them to attend to. The spectators had had their fun and had begun to leave. The match was abandoned. The two men left the stadium together.

'That was great, just great,' de Vries said 'I'm really hot now. Do you fancy a cool beer?'

'Yaaah, sure let's find a bar further into town.'

'Wow that was something that riot. Far better than the game which wasn't going anywhere. I'm Otto Kummel by the way and I live here in Dortmund.'

'I'm Koos de Vries, most people call me DV; I have come over from The Hague and it was bloody well worth it. Yes that riot was well worth coming for.'

They walked together to the halt from where they could get a bus into the centre. Along the journey, Kummel suddenly said:

'Next stop we get off, I know a good place.'

They stepped down from the bus and walked across to the Imperial bar in Kreuzestrasse. There were a few people in the bar in supporter's gear who had arrived from the abandoned football match and one or two regulars but it wasn't crowded. They ordered litre mugs of Konig Pilsner and sat down at a table.

'Do you follow Ajax regularly; have you been to away matches in other places?' Kummel asked.

'Yes, I like the way they play and I take a trip to away games whenever I can; it is a good way to visit other countries. I have been to France, England, Italy and Portugal so far.'

'Well, I have followed Dortmund for a while but I am less adventurous. I also like Ajax. I have only been to Belgium and The Netherlands. Easy trips quite nearby.'

They ordered more beers and chatted away about what work they did and what interests they had. They were beginning to enjoy their relaxed meeting. They couldn't help chuckling each time they remembered how the riot had built up so quickly after the two players were booked.

'So funny that referee staggering off with his bleeding head. The marshals were out in the middle surrounding him but they were too scared to bring him into the stands because of the booing and the missiles. The police had to fetch them.'

'Marvellous. I won't forget this afternoon for a long while DV.'

'Yaaah, the whole thing was epic, just epic, bloody great.'

'Let's go to Babuska's Kitchen and have something to eat,' Otto said, 'It is just over there,' pointing down the street.

'Babushka's is an institution-famous for its hearty Ukrainian cooking.'

'That will be just the job now we have had a few beers.'

The restaurant had an ambience all of its own which just avoided being Balalaika folksy. The walls were painted a bright cerulean blue, the tables and benches were in polished pine and the light fittings were recycled industrial pendants.

Thanks to the match being abandoned, it was still only early evening, the restaurant wasn't crowded and they were able to get a table.

De Vries said, 'Your guidance please Otto, on what is best to eat here.'

'Well, there are several variations of beef stews—the Ukraine bowl, the Odessa bowl, the Caucasus bowl and so on, they are all tasty but last time, I had the meatballs in Paprika sauce with Sauerkraut and roast potatoes and I tell you, it is damn good and I'm going to have it again.'

'Sounds good to me, I will have it too.'

'But first, more beers,' Kummel said and called to the waiter. When he arrived, they ordered four beers and the meatballs.

During their supper, they expanded on what they did and what they did away from work. After a bit of skirting around, de Vries mentioned his PVV activities. Kummel visibly relaxed and mentioned his own interest in Blood and Honour. They spent a good while comparing notes.

Kummel confessed to not much liking his boring life as an accountant and that he had always looked forward to the excitement of the weekend activities. De Vries said much the same, there was little interest in scaffolding, he only did it for the money. PVV with its cadre of like-minded 'soldiers' and the frequent aggressive actions offered him a total release.

He said that he had got into drugs a few years ago to lift himself but that he was trying to kick the habit now and pointed to his nostrils.

'I don't want this to get any worse, it is bad enough now. I have pretty well managed to stop and just use it occasionally. I find that I can get a similar high by joining in all our actions and serious rough stuff. I live on it.'

They talked on and readily compared their acts of violence. Kummel showed de Vries his Oyster knife and said that he had stabbed twelve youths at one demo—that was his record. De Vries countered by saying that he had put two youths into A & E and one into intensive care. The one that was in intensive care would not be the same again, so maybe he will limp off back to Turkey, he chortled.

'That was good fortune that riot,' de Vries said, 'otherwise we would not have met.'

'Yes, good fortune coming from a disastrous game.'

'I think we have a lot in common, Otto and you must come over and see me in The Hague - just come anyway, we don't need to wait for a Europa League match.'

'Yes but before any of that you should come over and join in our attack on the Turks in Bremen next weekend. We aim to give them a good beating to make them think again about staying in Germany.

We will be having a real clear out of those trash people. Our fellows will be delighted to meet a man from the PVV, a man of the same heart and with your record. Think about it, you will be welcome.'

They were thoroughly pleased with their day and their talk through the evening.

'We should have some Schnapps to finish,' Kummel said and he ordered two.

'Yaah and I will have a bit of this stuff,' de Vries said rolling a joint.

When they were ready to leave, Kummel insisted on paying the bill.

'This is my town,' he said, 'you can be in charge when I visit The Hague.'

'By the way, where are you staying?'

'I had not planned to stay; I will drive back to The Hague.'

'No, no, you don't DV, you can stay with me.'

18

Tomas Lopes da Silva lived in that comfortable top strata of Portuguese society. As head of the family bank, Banca Caixas, he was well known in international banking circles and was influential in the business world. He led an exemplary life much as would be expected of a senior member of a long-established leading family. He had been a councillor for many years and was now a senator.

He had been feted and decorated. He had been married for thirty years to a woman from an equally distinguished family and was not known to have strayed from the straight and narrow. The couple had three grown up children who were all doing well in their chosen fields. The two girls were doctors and the son was running the Madrid branch of Banca Caixas.

Tomas Lopes da Silva was a true pillar of high society.

But his past had been a bit different. He had grown into adulthood during the period when Salazar had controlled the country. During the last years of the regime, da Silva had become a Commandante in PIDE and had been active in working to maintain the totalitarian government.

Though he was destined for the family bank, his father had insisted that his son should be seen to do his bit to support Salazar and maintain the "beneficial" regime.

He had become the commanding officer of the brigade responsible for carrying out reprisals against any attacks on the military or PIDE officers made by emergent democrats and centrists. Against anyone daring to criticise or fight against the regime. His area of operational command was the north of the country, the mountainous region from Castelo Branco to Braganca. He was based at the army barracks in Serta.

Santa Cruz and Casals had been officers in his corps..

In the spring of 1967, a PIDE officer and three soldiers had been ambushed and killed in the village of Pampilhosa da Serra in the mountains east of Lousa. As would have been expected of him, da Silva would have to organise an appropriate reprisal. He had delegated the arrangements to Santa Cruz and Casals.

That had been a mistake. He had been appalled by the scale of the reprisal they had carried out. A busy cafe had been bombed and eleven people including two nine–year-old twin girls had been killed. Eight locals and three foreigners had been wiped out. The duo had exceeded their orders and should have been court-marshalled for their unnecessarily excessive and ill-judged action.

It should have been a national scandal but a D notice had been slapped on the already tightly controlled press. The outrage had been hushed up by the local command. There had been a behind-the-scenes whitewash enquiry into the disastrous action at the village.

Santa Cruz and Casals had been censured and ordered to keep a low profile. They had been moved sideways into supplies and maintenance. They had also been given medals for bravery and valour.

Lopes da Silva had continued to keep the whole affair under tight wraps and to hold it over the two officers to keep them under his influence. He had liked the idea of a dedicated duo who would have to do his bidding. He had kept them close to him for the years since the incident. They had become his own enforcers, directly employed to undertake unsavoury tasks..

After the fall of Salazar in 1968, Santa Cruz, Casals and most of the PIDE corps went "underground". The days of the Right were over for the time being. The country was embracing the new democracy with a fervour. Portugal had come back into the sunlight. People were visibly energised and cheerful. Life was good again. A whole generation had lived under repression and now they were moving forward.

But not everyone saw this as progress. The new government had become increasingly Socialist and da Silva, for one, didn't like what he saw. He regarded public spending on housing and education as a gross piece of fiscal mismanagement. The tax-funded health service-the SNS-was an outrage.

Why should he and others like him have to pay for it? Most of the people these subsidised services benefitted were undeserving immigrants, criminals, indolent beggars and druggies, complete no-hopers. Society's trash. Ordure.

He believed that the marked class divisions had been created for a purpose and he wanted them to be reinstated and reinforced. He and his family had always been part of the ruling class and he wanted that situation to be restored.

He firmly believed that people of his class were the only ones who knew how to run the country. Yes, they had made themselves rich in doing so but the country had been stable. As he saw it, everyone had benefitted then and now the country was going to the dogs.

The banker became a major contributor to funds for Far Right groups across Europe.

Groups that wanted to foster white supremacy, reverse immigration and prevent the cancerous spread of Islam. Day by day, he became more entrenched in his reactionary views. He wanted to increase the levels of funding; he wanted the groups to spread Europe wide.

He became more proactive and he was sufficiently influential to persuade others in Portugal, Germany and the Netherlands to act in a similar way-to embrace and fund the groups who would fight to de-stabilize the country and prepare the way for the return of a society they wished to see.

All of those whose support he had enlisted desired a return to the old order. They wanted the reinstatement of strong stable governments which were better for business, better for the economy. Better for their countries full stop. These men knew what was best.

They always had known; they had always been right. None of this drift towards flabby democracy. Firm fisted stability was what was needed again and they were prepared to pay what was necessary to achieve it. They willingly contributed to da Silva's funding scheme.

He required couriers in The Netherlands and Germany. He ordered Santa Cruz and Casals to enlist them. He wanted men like themselves, men who could act both as couriers and as enforcers.

Santa Cruz and Casals had the right connections; they were in touch with 'officers' in the groups and through them, found the men they needed. They enlisted de Vries and Kummel who would make the collections from BWD Bank Netherlands and Deutsch Bank Bremen.

The cash would be run through France and Spain to Lisbon for distribution. Banca Caixas would be the focal point. The couriers would take the cash boxes from the Dutch and German banks to Santa Cruz and Casals. De Vries and Kummel usually passed their boxes over at chosen rendezvous points outside Portugal.

Santa Cruz would choose out of the way hotels. Once the transfers had been made the ex PIDE men would drive the cash down to da Silva for distribution. They would also make the final distribution in Lisbon to the intermediaries for the groups.

Da Silva kept a tight control of the clandestine operations, nothing was recorded, nothing was openly visible. There would be no incriminating evidence. He gave his orders to Santa Cruz and Casals and they were the only ones in direct contact with him. He knew they would not dare to be disloyal.

But as the four men got more confident they began to get slack. They began to combine business with pleasure by arranging to meet at Euro football matches and then to make the transfers at designated places out of town. They became almost brazen enough to make the transfers in public view.

It had become a very smooth routine operation but now someone was taking advantage, someone had turned. Someone was helping himself.

At each transfer point, there might be one less box than expected. Nothing could be proved because, deliberately, nothing had been recorded. Nothing had ever been recorded, it would have been too dangerous to have any sort of paper trail. Santa Cruz and Casals discussed the situation between themselves and decided to keep a close eye on the others.

If their suspicions increased, they would have to deal with the guilty man. Da Silva would blame them for any shortcomings in the men they had themselves recruited and they could not afford to let that happen. They needed to strike first. Anyone on the take would have to be liquidated. Da Silva would be implacable in the vengeance he would take on his lieutenants if they failed him.

19

Santa Cruz and Casals needed to reflect on what they knew about their two recruits and they needed to think hard about whether they had made a mistake. They sat in the Bar Museo drinking strong coffee and brandies thinking out loud. What did they know of the backgrounds of those two?

De Vries and Hummel had told them that they had met each other at Ajax matches in Amsterdam and Dortmund and had become "match" buddies. They were keen to be sociable on their visits to Lisbon and had joined Santa Cruz and Casals after a Europa League match.

What started as a casual acquaintance became a regular get together. They had become a foursome for drinking after the games. They usually had a lot to drink, especially de Vries and Hummel. It was almost as if the two Northerners had been released from confinement.

They really went for it. As the alcohol took hold of them, they would often talk about their extra mural activities. They both belonged to extremist groups and were proud of their activities joining in the often violent protests and organised brawls. They would talk about these activities in lurid detail.

They were more interested in the physical violence than any intellectual ideal but they would have called themselves Right wing, far-Right if they had to admit to any kind of political affiliation.

That had seemed enough they had seemed good candidates. They had felt back then that the new men were sufficiently attuned to their own ideas to warrant recruiting them as the two couriers. They were doers not thinkers-they didn't want thinkers who might complicate the set up.

It would be unlikely that de Vries and Kummel would ask awkward questions; they were likely to obey their instructions, they liked the pay on offer. Both were single so neither had dependents who might get in the way and ask awkward questions.

Both had powerful cars which they would need for bringing the funds down from The Netherlands and Germany and they both loved driving. They had seemed in most ways perfect.

'Yes, I think that is a fair summary, Jorge and I think it shows we may have been too quick to recruit and befriend them and far too trusting. We were not careful enough, we allowed drinking pals to become enmeshed in the organisation. We should have made better checks.'

They weren't reaching any definite conclusion on which of the couriers might be the culprit. Both seemed to be equally capable of doing the dirty. They were both nasty pieces of work as they recognised themselves to be, especially Casals in his PIDE days. They knew what it was like to be off the rails.

They thought about each man in turn.

De Vries looked every bit the scaffolder. He usually dressed in jeans, studded leather jacket and fake DMs. He was every bit the overgrown bovver boy. Strongly built, he had crew-cut blond hair and fully tattooed arms. He had a pockmarked face, mean-looking eyes and a full blond moustache.

His nostrils were a bit damaged, presumably from his Cocaine use. He had three pointed silver rings on the middle fingers of his right hand.

'My knuckle dusters,' he had said with pride 'always ready for a fight.' He had told them that he lived on his own and apart from his four employees had few regular friends in everyday life. His friends were in his alternative life, the PVV and he joined them at weekend rallies to noisily demonstrate in favour of White Supremacy, shout anti-Islamic slogans and smash up the windows of shops run by Pakistanis and Turks.

He had enthusiastically joined in organised attacks on coloured youths and said he had put two of them into A&E and one into intensive care himself.

He had said he wasn't much of a thinker, he didn't read the serious newspapers, he preferred the tabloids and the PVV pamphlets that promulgated hate. He had taken these views on board and thought the immigrants were scum who should be cleared out by any means necessary.

He wasn't interested in reading books. He could read but it wasn't a pleasure for him. He had been expelled from school for consistently attacking other boys and his education had suffered. He liked watching TV and playing video games, the more violent the game the better. He often played online through the night with one of his PVV friends.

When asked whether he knew someone in Germany who might also be suitable, he had suggested Kummel.

Otto Kummel was a different kettle of fish. He presented himself as a mild mannered jobbing accountant who worked for a number of private clients. He looked completely inoffensive in his grey suits and polished black shoes. His face was round, his black hair was centre parted and pomaded and he wore round black framed spectacles.

He portrayed himself to be a regular innocent clean living fellow. He was a bit old-fashioned looking and had that weird tick, otherwise he was unremarkable. But he had said that he had always felt marginalised, ever since he was the class swot at school. Teachers liked him, his fellow pupils didn't.

He had told them that he lived on his own and had always had difficulty in making women friends. He thought that the involuntary spasmic jerking of his head had put some off. In fact, he had difficulty in making any friends. He believed that people often thought he was weird; they didn't understand that his physical difficulties were outside his control.

He had a few acquaintances through his business but they were not close friends. He had said that he had often felt lonely which was why it was so good to meet up with them. "The four musketeers" he had declared them to be.

He had told them that he was only able to express himself fully when he joined the Blood and Honour group for their activities. There they had taken him at face value and his physical peculiarities were accepted without comment. Many of them had peculiarities.

The increasing bitterness fermented by his loneliness found its relief in the attacks on the Turkish immigrants. He had thrived on the camaraderie offered by his violent friends. He had shown Santa Cruz and Casals his Oyster knife with the swastika carved into the wooden handle.

He said that he felt it was like in that story—Jekyll and Hyde. He could feel the personality switch each time and it excited him. He felt himself change from his normal measured life to someone who was out of control and ready to feed on violence.

Both of them had come "alive" when they had met to pass the Transit boxes and receive their own salary payments. They had found that they got on well enough to have social meetings after the business had been done. Both of the men had said that they enjoyed their meetings and staying the night at the different hotels that Santa Cruz would choose. They looked forward to those special evenings when they could let themselves go. It was part of their vital alternative life.

The two PIDE men remembered all this and needed to point themselves in the right direction. Who should they concentrate on? Who had turned? One of them? Both of them?

Casals took the lead:

'Well, where have we got to Xavier? I have to say I am still unable to say which one we should chase.'

'De Vries is the more obvious, I think,' Santa Cruz said 'Everyone knows scaffolders are brutes. He had always been doing more violence than Kummel. Don't be fooled, Jorge, by his dumb heavy act. He knows what he is doing, he isn't that stupid. I think he is the one to watch.'

'No, I don't think that is quite right. Kummel is the one stabbing people with his Oyster knife. He is no angel and he is the cleverer of the two. Damn it, he is an accountant too so maybe he is the one who has worked out a scam? Yes Xavier, my money is on Kummel not de Vries.'

'Maybe but we should watch them both closely until we can be sure. We can't afford to get it wrong, the consequences would be dire for us.'

20

Hotel Esplendido in Barragem do Cabril was a small family run hotel. It mainly catered for fishermen going for trout in the nearby river Zezere or for those intending to do some walking in the hills and mountains around. The family and staff were friendly and helpful. They were able to suggest good spots for fishing and advise on the relative ease or difficulty of the mountain trails.

They printed out the local weather forecasts and pinned them up daily on the notice board in reception. They would provide packed lunches for any guests who asked for them. It was a well-run cheerful place to stay.

The three Dutch brothers staying there back in the spring of 1967 were walkers. They tried to meet up for a short holiday together every couple of years. This was to be their fourth holiday together. They had stayed at the hotel four years before, liked it and decided to stay again.

They usually chose to meet for their holidays together in the spring as the mountains were beautiful and everything was fresh then. There weren't many visitors to spoil the peace and quiet either.

The two eldest, Joost and Markus worked on engineering projects for Shell International operating out of Lisbon. Kees, the youngest of them had a good job as a transit manager at the container port in Rotterdam. He would fly down to Lisbon, they would pick him up at the airport and they would go off together from there.

Sometimes, Joost and Markus's wives had joined them but now that they had children, it had become more difficult. They couldn't very well take young children up and down mountains. The wives were phlegmatic about it. Let the men go on their own, they thought, we will have our proper family holidays in the summer.

Walking in the Serra de Alvelos was hard going over rough terrain but they were enjoying the clear pine scented air and the sight of Eagles and Griffon Vultures circling above as well as the Purple Orchids and Iris growing everywhere about.

They had seen wild goats and deer in the mountains and in the forests they had seen wild boar. It was so wonderful and liberating. It was a joy to be out of the cities and up there in the mountains even though their feet had become blistered on the second day.

They had left their stuffy offices and tedious routines behind to have four days of total freedom. It was healthy and it was exhilarating; they loved being in the wild.

On the third day, they headed west to the Serra de Lousa. It was rocky terrain with patches of low growing grass and gorse. The views were wonderful right across to Figueira and the Atlantic. Stunning. As they were pointing out to each other the various landmarks that could be seen, they noticed two jeeps on a track below them.

They themselves must have been seen because the jeeps turned towards them and raced up the hill. There were three men in each jeep. When they reached the brothers, the officer in the first jeep ordered them to halt. He aggressively demanded to know who they were and what they were doing.

Joost told him that they were Dutch visitors and were taking a walking holiday. They were staying at the hotel in Barragem and had been there for three days.

The officer demanded to see their papers and when they had offered their passports to him, he examined each one carefully. He passed the Passports back to Joost and spoke in broken English.

'Good. These are O.K. Enjoy your walking Dutchmen but be careful. We are here looking for people, bandit people, no good people, criminal people. Have you seen? People with guns? Suspicious people? We will find them and we will kill them all.'

Joost said they hadn't seen anyone at all which was why they liked walking in the Serra at this time of the year.

The officer seemed satisfied if disappointed. He nodded, climbed back into his jeep and the patrol drove off.

'Well that was a surprise,' Joost said 'I wouldn't like to get on the wrong side of that bunch. He made me seriously nervous.'

'What were they talking about anyway?' Kees asked 'I hadn't heard that there were dangerous bandits in these mountains.'

'Yes that has spoilt the day a bit.' Markus chipped in. 'Still there is always tomorrow and, as it will the last day of our holiday, maybe we should take it a bit easier and avoid the higher mountains.'

The brothers had always planned their holidays carefully, so that they would be exploring different terrain each day. One day, they would be in the forested slopes to the South, the next in the barren mountains to the North and so on.

The pattern was that they would start off early, get in a good few miles of walking then stop to eat a simple lunch at a village cafe. Afterwards, they would continue on their route in a loop ultimately ending back at the village again. From there they would call for a taxi to take them back to Barragem and their hotel. Yes, they had worked out a good formula and it had proved its worth over the years.

In the evenings, they would talk about the family. Joost and Marcus would show photos of their growing children to uncle Kees. They would just enjoy chatting about life in general and chatting as brothers do. They would have a supper prepared by the no nonsense cook who would make nourishing casseroles of goat or wild boar.

It wasn't a hotel for vegetarians.

They would have a carafe of the local wine and sometimes a brandy but would go to their rooms quite early so as to be up and about first thing. They met for a simple breakfast of the country bread with cheese or jam and strong coffees.

The waiter would bring each of them a bottle of water and an apple to keep them going through the morning. Refreshed, they would set out to follow the route they had worked out the previous evening. Kees would take charge of the map.

This day, which was the last of their short vacation they had reached Pampilhosa de Serra, a small but picturesque village on the river Zezere After they had cooled their feet in the river, they looked inside the church, walked around the small shaded square and sat down for lunch at cafe Zezere.

They were surprised that most of the tables had been taken but it was a Sunday and a fine day to be out. Family groups were having lunch and some of the younger children were playing together and paddling. Most people were sitting outside with just a few watching the football on the TV inside.

Two fishermen were sitting together at another table. Their rods were propped up against a spare chair, their nets and tackle bags on the ground beside it.

The pretty young waitress came over to their table to take their orders. All three of them ordered a litre glass of cool draught beer and Frango e batatas fritas from the bar menu. There weren't many choices on the short menu but they all felt that the chicken would be better than the steak. They had had enough of tough steaks.

The day was pleasantly warm-cloud cover had masked the scorching sun and there was a gently cooling breeze.

A basket of bread and some olives arrived. They started on the bread and were enjoying their cool beers. They congratulated themselves on the choice of cafe for their simple lunch stop.

That was the last they knew. The last they knew of anything. They didn't even hear the bang.

21

In Lisbon, the case had stalled a bit and they had no new leads. They had found the four men who had acted as couriers, they had learnt something about their backgrounds and had discovered where they had met together at least three times, in Castagnede, Haro and Lisbon but they had little more to go on than that. They knew that four of them had met in Lisbon and three of them in Castagnede and Haro.

They needed more evidence to flesh out the picture. They decided to try another brain-storming session. It was to be a free-flow session; anything goes, no matter how wild it might at first seem.

Expecting a long session, da Costa had asked Gloria to arrange sandwiches and wine as before. They could just about manage coffees themselves.

They came up with many of the same ideas but eliminated some of them. They were looking for new angles.

A young DC suggested that football might be the link. They had found out that Kummel was an Ajax supporter. Well anyway, they knew he had been to two recent matches. Ajax Amsterdam was also on the doorstep for de Vries, it would have taken him just an hour or so to get to the stadium so maybe he was also a fan? Maybe they met at matches? If Hummel and de Vries met at matches, how and where did the others fit in?

They decided to focus on this. The young DC was a football follower himself and knew what to look for. He suggested that they should look through the schedules of tournament matches played in Lisbon and Oporto over the last few years and specifically visits made by Ajax Amsterdam. The other team members suggested that he should take the lead as he knew what he was looking for.

He found there had been two Champions League home games between Ajax and FC Porto in Oporto and Ajax and Lisboa FC in Lisbon. Getting to those matches couldn't have been easier for Santa Cruz and Casals but would the other two have followed Ajax that far? Yes, perhaps if the money transfers were made at the same times. It might be something to hang on to and everyone agreed it would be worth exploring further.

Half of the PJ team went over to Oporto the next day to show the photos around in bars commonly used by football fans. They called at Bar Sporting, Bar 24/7, John Bull Pub, Bar Futebol and half a dozen others but enquires drew a disappointing blank. If they had stayed drinking in Oporto, no-one had noticed them.

The team making the bar to bar visits in Lisbon had more success. The men had been recognised by the staff in two bars in the Alfama district. The bar tender in Bar Legende recognised two of the four men in the photo but said they had stayed just for a couple of drinks. One of them had insisted that they should all try a new Dutch Lager which they didn't yet have at Legende. They had finished their Sagres and then moved off to try to find the new lager elsewhere.

In the bar Esportivo, the staff thought there had been five men sitting together and that they had been talking loudly and animatedly. One of the men had had an involuntary twitch, which caused his head to jerk to the side. The bar tender and waiters found it impossible not to watch though they knew it was wrong of them.

Another of the men had fully tattooed arms but that wasn't unusual, they got quite a few like that in the cafe. Yes-the four men in the photos and one other. He was taller and bigger than the others they remembered. The barman with the most to say said they had drunk a great amount of the new Haag Pils that had recently arrived and some wine—more than the average amount drunk by groups of fans after matches. Two of them had gone outside to smoke a few times.

Da Costa and Tremaine who had made the enquiry at Cafe Esportivo phoned Gloria Esteban and Sam Redwood.

'Come to cafe Esportivo. Our men came here,' Da Costa said. 'We are sitting outside and I have ordered cool beers.'

When the other pair arrived and had had a refreshing drink of their beers, da Costa summed up what they now knew.

'So, we know that they have met socially in Lisbon at least twice and maybe all five of them had met together if the original photographer was part of the group. For the time being, I think we should work on the assumption that the fifth man was part of the group and probably had been the photographer. It will be a priority now to find out what we can about him.'

They discussed what they knew and thought it would be likely that after their drinking sessions in the bars they would have eaten in restaurants nearby. They thought that the men would not have wanted to walk far after drinking the amount of alcohol the barmen had described.

In any case, had they wanted to go further, they would have had to walk out of the district to find a taxi. A taxi to take five people would have been very difficult to find. Difficult anyway but especially difficult on those busy nights. They would assume therefore that they had eaten in restaurants within easy reach of the bars.

They knew the group had eaten at AlfamaMar where else might they have been? Had they been seen to meet others who might be involved in the trafficking?'

They decided to make door to door enquiries at Alfama restaurants when they opened for lunch. They split into groups of two as before with the DCs making up two other teams. They were to ask at restaurants, bars and cafes in all the streets and alleyways in the district. That proved to be another disappointment. The men were not recognised in any of the restaurants or other bars which were open.

'That was disappointing,' da Costa said 'but not all of the restaurants have opened yet. We should come back this evening and check out those that had been closed.'

'Yes that would be the best thing to do,' Redwood agreed.

Gloria had an evening engagement but da Costa, Redwood and Tremaine agreed that they would meet again at the Bar Esportivo at 8:00.

22

The way the operation worked was that da Silva would contact his counterparts in the other four banks and set a date for the collections to be made.

Each of the banks had two senior clerks who had been brought into the loop. They would have become part of the mechanism on the promise of preferment and a share of the cash. It was likely too that they would also have approved of the purpose, funding the extremist groups.

Their job was to siphon off cash when customers deposited it. Not every time a deposit was made but in a randomised frequency and only when the two clerks were on duty together. They would carry out the required checking procedures but these would be a charade. It would appear that the process had been in accordance with banking rules but it would not have been.

In each of the banks, the two clerks would supervise each other in the opening and closing of security doors and in the opening up of deposit boxes in the vaults. They would each have the keys and know the codes. Once they were in the vaults and had opened the boxes, they would skim 20% of the notes off the top and replace them with counterfeit notes of equivalent value which were then placed below the legal notes in the deposit boxes.

There was a sound logic to this; no customer ever took out all of the deposited cash, they took only portions of it. They would not discover that they had been duped. In any case, most of the cash deposited had been made on the Black otherwise it could have been put into normal accounts. The depositors would not want to draw attention to themselves by making a fuss. It was pretty well a foolproof operation.

The skimmed-off notes were put into Transit boxes and held in the banks ready for distribution. The whole procedure had been made much easier with the introduction of the Euro currency. The bank notes brought in by the customers might come from several different countries but they were valid throughout the whole of Europe. No need nowadays for potentially dangerous slip-ups with currency exchanges.

When the funds were in place, da Silva would contact Santa Cruz and Casals, his own lieutenants who would then contact de Vries and Kummel to tell them when to collect the transit boxes from the Dutch and German banks. More locally, Santa Cruz would collect from Banca Sociedad Alto in Lisbon and Casals from the branch of Banca Escorial across the Spanish border in Merida.

They had done this time and time again. The funds from Portugal and Spain would be taken direct to Banca Caixas. The funds from the Dutch and German banks would be picked up at a transfer point.

The three or four of them would meet at the designated place, chosen by Santa Cruz, where de Vries and Hummel would pass over their Transit boxes. These would then be taken down to Lisbon either by Casals or Santa Cruz or both of them.

Da Silva had ordered a pick up but this time neither Santa Cruz nor Casals could get hold of Otto Kummel. It was unexpected and strange, Kummel's mobile number just wasn't ringing out. Surely he could see on the screen who was trying to get hold of him? Was he deliberately avoiding them?

Had Kummel noticed the change in the attitude of the two PIDE men? Had he realised that they had become suspicious of him and of de Vries and that he was under scrutiny? He certainly would have known that that he would be hunted down if he was discovered to have taken some of the cash. He would have known that da Silva would order the severest punishment.

Santa Cruz phoned de Vries and asked him to go over to Dortmund to find out where Kummel was. Not to do anything, anything at all, just to find out if he was there in Dortmund.

He knew Kummel's address - they all had each other's addresses and mobile numbers. He made the two hour journey and called at the apartment. He rang the bell. There was no answer. He had sat drinking coffees in the bar opposite for a while in case Kummel turned up. He didn't. Kummel's apartment was number 3B.

He rang the bell of apartment 3A across the landing. When the speakeasy answering system came alive, he apologised for ringing the bell but said he was looking for Otto Kummel and asked if he had been seen recently. The elderly sounding neighbour said:

'No, I haven't seen him for a while nor have I heard his ghastly loud music either, thank God. And don't disturb me again, I was having a siesta.'

De Vries would have preferred to catch Kummel unawares but he didn't have an alternative now other than to call his mobile number. He dialled it. After a few rings, the recorded message stated that the number was not receiving incoming calls.

He phoned Casals and told him that Kummel did not appear to be in Dortmund, could not be traced and that his mobile was no longer active. He had gone AWOL.

Casals thought about this for a while then he called Santa Cruz to give him the news.

'Look Jorge,' Santa Cruz said 'I think we had better meet to discuss this. We should meet at Bar Museo at six. I will see you then.'

Both of them had time to think about what might be happening. By the time they met at the bar, they had both become nervous.

They picked up a beer at the bar and then moved outside to a table under a tree at the edge of the cafe's seating area. Though the cafe wasn't busy and there was no-one to overhear him, Casals asked in an urgent half-whisper like a stage prompt:

'Do you think Kummel has tumbled to us suspecting him? Do you think he has disappeared in order to cover his tracks? What do you think? Where is he?'

'I don't know,' Santa Cruz replied 'but I'm worried. If he realises that we suspect him, he may try to get at us and get his retaliation in first. He knows that da Silva would order us to zap him if he was found to be helping himself. If he got rid of us, he would be safer. He knows that only we have contact with da Silva and only we know who Kummel is and where to find him. If he got rid of us, he probably wouldn't be found.

He has money and could go anywhere he wanted to stay safe. He wouldn't stop short of a killing or two. We know what he is capable of, he is a vicious bastard.'

'Jesus, you don't think that, do you? What coming after us, coming after us?' Casals said urgently.

'Yes and I think we had better be watching our backs.'

Both of the men now looked more worried and the Spaniard had started sweating profusely and shifting in his seat. They had talked themselves into a panic. Kummel could be on the move and on his way to hit them before they could hit him. They decided to take cover and to ask da Silva to delay the collection date, spinning him the story that they had both picked up a nasty dose of Flu and would be out of action for a while.

They would see shadows everywhere. But how could they be sure? Maybe it wasn't Kummel who was on the take and it was de Vries and all that stuff he had said about Kummel had been a smoke screen. Maybe it was de Vries who was after them? Maybe they had got together and were both coming. Casals had said.

Santa Cruz looked as if he was about to feint.

'Holy shit. Jesus. Mary mother of God!' he exclaimed. Then he said:

'I'm going to disappear and you should too. We must shut our apartments here in Lisbon and just go. Go to separate places. It will be better to lie low individually. We would be much more noticeable together. Don't phone me unless it is a dire emergency and I won't phone you. No contact, no contact with anyone, anyone at all. We must become invisible, untraceable.'

He was the more nervous of the two and intended to put hundreds of miles behind him and flee to England. In England, he would be safe. No-one would look for him there.

But Casals had laid a smokescreen. It wasn't Kummel who had helped himself, it was Casals. He had become greedy and lazy. He wished to get out from the operation and just retire to somewhere pleasant. He had had enough of his relationship with Santa Cruz, he wanted out of that too.

His old comrade and lover would never suspect him of helping himself to the money. He was cleverly deceitful and fuelled Santa Cruz's suspicions of de Vries and Kummel. Kummel had played into his hands marvellously by going AWOL.

With the money that was in the two Transit boxes, he could pretty well choose to live anywhere he liked. But he would have to wait a while; he would have to lie low for now.

He knew how long a reach da Silva had and he was now very nervous that he could be killed. If da Silva became aware of his operation being compromised or exposed, he had other enforcers who would do his bidding, who would hunt down and exterminate anyone who had crossed the boss.

Casals took to the hills. He knew the mountainous areas of the Serra de Alvelos and the Serra da Lousa from his time in PIDE. He felt he would be safer in an area he knew well. He knew most of the back roads and tracks throughout the area.

He had used them when he had been hunting for partisans. He knew where the remote places were. It didn't take him long to find a possible hideaway. A peasant farmer—a pequeno agriculto agreed to let him have a shepherd's hut for minimal rent. It was basic, just an earth floored hovel but it was dry and he could shelter there.

The farmer also agreed to supply some food from his small holding. Basic stuff like eggs, beans, potatoes and his home made wine and Serra cheese. Casals was pretty sure he would be safe, he was pretty sure he had made a good choice. He kept himself confined and only went out for a short time in the early morning and at dusk.

He told himself he had to do this, he had to stay careful. Completely out of sight. He would take his exercise walks only at night when there was a bright moon to see by.

Three weeks later when he was delivering some eggs, the farmer found Casals dead in his hideaway. He had been killed by garrotting. The farmer knew about garrotting. Years ago, two of his son's friends had been executed by PIDE whilst they had been hunting rabbits in the mountains.

They had been severely tortured and killed. He looked without compassion at the dead man then walked down into the village and called the police from the phone in the cafe

The police sergeant who drove out to the hovel, secured the scene as best he could and interviewed the small holder. The farmer told him of the man's arrival five weeks earlier and his stated need for a place to lie low. The farmer didn't care much about which side of the law he was on. The hovel was empty.

The man had offered him cash for the use of it, so what was he to do? How was he to know if there was anything fishy? Maybe the man was hiding from a husband who he had wronged? Maybe he was hiding from his wife? Some women could be ferocious; real harridans.

He didn't know why the man had come. How could he know? Anyway, the cash was welcome. Did the sergeant know how little he had to live on? The state pension paid a pittance. Not like your fat salary. Did he want to begrudge an old man a bit of extra cash? What was the world coming to? Did no-one have any respect for the elderly anymore? In my day—

When the SOC team arrived, the sergeant was relieved to be able to get away. SOC officers did their act on the body and on the hovel. Apart from the fact that the man had obviously been murdered, they found nothing. An ambulance was called and it carted the body to Covilha.

There, the Post Mortem showed that Casals had been tortured before he was killed.

Had he been tortured to make him give out wanted information? What information?

The police were in the dark, they could not establish a motive for the killing. They weren't going to waste time on a fuller investigation. It was what it was. The man didn't seem to be important and no-one had been listed as missing. The case would just fester in a file in the local police station in Serta.

A week later, Kummel telephoned Santa Cruz. He said he had had a complete breakdown and had taken himself off to Bad Steben Spa to recuperate. He couldn't really remember the start of his collapse, it just suddenly overwhelmed him.

At the Spa, he had had to surrender his mobile phone that was part of the relaxation plan. No contact with the outside world, no radio, TV or phones were permitted. He had completely surrendered himself to their wellness regime.

He had stayed there for three weeks and it had put him back on track. He was back in his apartment in Dortmund now. When he asked how things were, Santa Cruz said the whole operation was in meltdown. When he was asked where he was, he replied that he was not in Portugal and that he should not contact him again or give his mobile number to anyone else.

The breakdown of the operation was inconvenient and embarrassing for da Silva. He had contacted his counterparts and the funds had not been collected. It was inexplicable. He telephoned Santa Cruz and demanded that he should come to Lisbon to answer questions face to face.

He would freeze Santa Cruz's account at Banca Caixas if he did not come immediately from wherever he was. He would have him hunted down if he did not come. And he had better get his two henchmen to come too.

'I mean it, Santa Cruz; you get here immediately.'

23

Alfredo, Gloria's live-in boyfriend of four years was away in Barcelona for the week at an international exhibition and conference on recent developments in I.T. He was in charge of I.T. in Allianz Portugal one of the bigger insurance companies. Gloria was pleased he was away and that she had the place to herself, she needed to think.

Things weren't going at all well between them. They were having frequent rows. She was fed up with the way Alfredo was taking her for granted, not making any effort, always saying he was tired from overwork. She reckoned she worked harder and longer hours than he did. He had become dull and boring.
They rarely had sex now and that was the main damn reason she had allowed him into her life. He never wanted to go out. He just wanted to flop down in front of the TV and watch sport. She felt too constrained. She felt he was stifling the life out of her.

She badly needed to break out. Yes, she damn well would go to her old friend Estella's party on Friday. They had been at school together and had kept in touch over the years. Yes, she would get out of the rut and join Estella's group of high-living friends for the evening. She knew she was attractive and wanted to see if her charms still worked. She would wear that slinky low-cut midnight blue dress.

When she arrived at the villa in Restello, she was greeted enthusiastically by Estella's husband Juan. Juan was a minor aristocrat and moneyed to the hilt. Their parties were always lavish, even over-the-top. Receiving an invitation was highly desirable.

'Come and meet these delicious people.' He took her arm, gave her a glass of Lanson and propelled her through the colonnaded courtyard towards the first group of guests he could see who were standing next to the fountain. He made the introductions then peeled off to greet someone else.

The group of three men and a woman rudely ignored her and continued to talk about sport and the upcoming Winter Olympics. God knows where that event was going to be or when it was going to be or what the hell it was anyway. Gloria didn't give a damn about it.

She glazed over. God almighty—all this time waiting for a party and they are talking about sport! No doubt it will be football next and then Formula One. Jesus!

She needed to get away from them and seeing a young man standing on his own under one of the Palm trees, she went over. She had noticed that he had been looking at her.

'Hi, I'm Gloria Esteban.'

'Pleased to meet you. I'm Antonio da Silva.'

He took two glasses from a passing waitress and passed one to Gloria. She realised that he had already had a few. He became excitedly talkative and wanted to know all about her. She said she was a secretary in a law firm and had worked there for the last four years.

Da Silva had heard of the firm. They had at one stage acted for one of the family to sort out an internal row.

'Oh, there are always problems in my family—never known it to be otherwise. Totally dysfunctional.'

The canapés were exceptional and must have been seriously expensive. As they came around, they took some and again some more of the choice bits. They did the same as the drinks came around. The band had become louder and though they were standing close together, they found that couldn't hold a proper conversation where they were.

They decided to go with the flow and mingle with the dancers for a stint. They squeezed their way over to the marble floor. Gloria liked the way he held her. He moved easily without the pushing and shoving Alfredo went in for. The music was good, they both danced well, it was enjoyable. After a lot of dancing, he asked if she had had enough of the party and whether she would like to go to the Casino. She looked uncertain.

'Oh, don't worry about money, I have an account there, at Lisbon that is. We will play the tables together.'

Even though he had had quite a bit to drink, he insisted that he could drive to the casino. He had parked his Lancia close to the entrance gates of the villa. They got in and set off for Casino Lisboa. Set beside the Tejo in the Parque de Nacoes the building was huge.

All glass and suspension structure it looked like it had been designed by someone who had worked with Richard Rogers. Whoever had been the designer, it must have cost a bomb. The doorman recognised Antonio and took the car keys. He would have the Lancia parked in the reserved spaces.

Antonio took her arm and they went in. The interior was ostentatiously glitzy. A brittle sort of space too impersonal and intimidating, she thought. They went over to one of the bars. He ordered a bottle of Krug and asked for it to be brought to them.

He guided her through to the huge room with the tables reserved for the bigger money players. There was a low buzz in the room, which was punctuated by the calls of the croupiers and the gasps of the punters.

They played at Roulette. He played, she stood by his side. She suggested numbers, he placed counters on them. She favoured red, more her colour than black, she thought. They won a modest amount over an hour or so and decided to quit whilst still on top. It was only supposed to be a bit of fun, they weren't in it to make money or to lose a lot for that matter.

'Tapas bar?' he asked.

'Yes a good idea, Antonio.'

They had only eaten canapés at the party and they needed something more to balance the alcohol.

They moved up to the Tapas bar and took a table next to the glass skin of the building. They could see the lights by the waterside below and some boats moving about. They grazed on a delicious selection of the small dishes and enjoyed the Champagne which they drank slowly.

Maybe he is a bit of a loner, Gloria thought because he was really giving her his attention. They talked about themselves and their friends without giving away any secrets and soon found it was one-thirty in the morning. He suggested that they should have a nightcap and ordered brandies.

When they had finished them, he asked her whether she would allow him to drive her home.

'Yes thanks, I would like that.'

His driving was erratic and Gloria was thankful that there weren't many cars about. It would be embarrassing if he were to be pulled over and she had to give the police her name too. God, just think of the teasing and laughter there would be at the station.

They reached Gloria's apartment block in the Chiado and took the lift to the fourth floor. Once inside, she said she needed more coffee and that she would make some. He sat down on the long settee.

In the kitchen, she realised how much she had enjoyed the evening. Antonio was good looking and courteous, she was definitely interested in him, she would see how the night developed.

When she came back with the coffee, he was flat out and had begun to snore.

24

He was mortified the next morning. How could he have been so rude? He apologised profusely, asked for Gloria's mobile number and rushed out. At 11:00, she got a call. It was Antonio.

'Look, please may I make try to make amends, will you have lunch with me?'

Why not, she thought, maybe I can even discover a bit about "the firm". She agreed that he would pick her up at 1:00.

'Shall we go to Tahine? It is nearby and we can walk there though the park.'

She knew where it was but said she hadn't been there; of course she hadn't, she knew it was expensive and Alfredo would not spend that sort of money. Ever. He was tight-fisted and mean, apart from everything else.

Antonio da Silva arrived exactly on time and she was also ready. They took the lift down, turned left and walked towards the restaurant. It was very impressive. It had been the palazzo of a well-known family before they had sold it to a prominent restauranteur. There was a large Baroque fountain in the tropically planted entrance court.

Four mermaids spouted water up to a regal Neptune in the centre. The walls of the interior were covered in eighteenth century tiles-the famous Azulejos from the Royal factory. Sumptuous. A completely intact and very special interior. They were given a good table next to the open court. The gentle breeze would keep them cool.

Antonio said he was feeling a bit delicate and would just have sparkling water, she should have whatever she would like.

'Water is fine by me today, thank you,' she said with a smile.

He ordered two bottles of Pedras Salgadas and some slices of lemon.

They looked at the menu but it began to defeat them; he wasn't focussing that well through his hangover.

'Let us have their specialities,' he said. 'If we both have the same, we won't get dish envy.'

'Good idea, you choose,' said Gloria.

The waiter arrived to take their order, Smoked Eel, Caviar and beetroot followed by Quail with quinces and wild funghi. It would all be delicious and they could take their time eating. It was and they did.

They talked generally and relaxedly about their families, where they had gone to school, how they had both come to know Juan and Estella, whether they had any other mutual friends and about things they liked to do. It was easy to talk, they were on the same wave length.

They talked on long after they had finished eating until Antonio realised that they were the only people left in the restaurant. He summoned the waiter and asked for the bill. He paid it and she noticed he had left a generous tip. Alfredo would never have done that either, she thought.

They walked back through the park again.

'I have really enjoyed our lunch, Gloria and I hope I will be able to tempt you out again.'

'Yes, Antonio I would love to be tempted.'

Three days later, he phoned again and asked if she could be free for lunch on Saturday. She said yes. She would like that. He said he would pick her up at midday and suggested that she might wear something casual, they would be going to the seaside.

On the day, he parked across the road and rang up to Gloria's apartment.

She came down looking very nautical in espadrilles, knee length navy blue shorts and a blue striped top.

'Wow you look great.'

'We are going to Atlantica in Peniche, have you been there? Terrific seafood.'

She said she hadn't, she knew it had a good reputation and she also knew it was very expensive.

When they arrived at Peniche, Gloria suggested that they take a short walk before lunch so that she could see the famous tube waves loved by the surfistas at the Praia dos Supertubos. They looked to her to be frighteningly big waves and they saw more surfers were falling off their boards than those who managed to stay on.

There were a lot of people enjoying the sport and more arriving all the time. More spectators too. It was an animated noisy scene with the crash of the waves and the crowds clapping and cheering the successful surfers. When they had seen enough, they walked on towards their lunch at Atlantica.

The restaurant was on the promontory at Peniche. The waves of the Atlantic washed over the rocks at each side. The white painted lighthouse gleamed in the sun. It was a marvellous location, almost too good, almost too perfect. They walked through the wrought iron gateway covered in bright Bougainvillea into to a vine covered court. The Maître recognised Antonio and took them to their table. He had booked one which he knew would offer some privacy.

'May I suggest that we have their sharing seafood platter? It is the dish they are best known for, it will have everything under the sun.'

'That sounds perfect,' Gloria replied. 'I'm hungry.'

When the waiter came, Antonio ordered the seafood speciality, a bottle of Vadio Branca Bairrada and a bottle of Luso water.

Having commented on the beauty of the setting and the particular smell of the sea, Gloria sensed that he wanted to tell her something. He looked at her quizzically as if inviting her to start. She blushed a little and confessed that she was an officer in the P J and not what she said she was at Estella's party.

'Sure,' he said, 'I knew you weren't a secretary, Estella told me.'

He seemed to want to get something out but was also hesitant. Then he started in a gush:

'My family own Banca Caixas and have done for generations. Currently, my uncle Lopes is in charge. His brother Faustino was my father. He worked in the bank as well when he was alive but he was side-lined and never allowed into the core of "the firm". He was paid a lot to do very little, to keep out of the way. He died three years ago.

I have been treated in the same way. I have too been side-lined. Yes, I have a high salary and I head up a bureau but it just handles PR and advertising. "Not exactly central to affairs" as they say. My father had seen and I have seen the bank taking a wrong path. I know that Banca Caixas is linked with extremist groups.

It has acted as bankers for the Right since even before Salazar. Its activities are anti-democratic and almost certainly criminal. Even now the bank is funding new Rightest groups wherever they appear like Chega here in Portugal.

I want it to be stopped. I can no longer stand by and see my family ruining people's lives and making themselves richer by doing so. I don't know who to tell in order to put a stop to it. I believe that many of the higher ranking prosecutors are in my uncle's pay and everyone knows there is a network of corrupt police.

When Estella told me that a pretty police woman was going to be at the party, I thought maybe I could tell her. Tell you that is, Gloria. Can you help? Are there people in the PJ you can trust?'

She wasn't at all surprised by his story about the activities of the bank. It confirmed what they had already discovered. She looked hard at him and gave what she hoped was a reassuring smile.

'Yes, I can help Antonio and I would like to do so. We will investigate thoroughly and do whatever is necessary to put a stop to the illegal funds. And no-one but my Supertintendente and I will know where the intelligence came from, I promise you. You will not be compromised. I will make it my personal mission.'

Now that he had got that burden off his chest, they were more able to enjoy their lunch, some more general conversation and basking in the warmth of the shaded sun. Antonio made more flattering comments about how Gloria looked and how delightful she was to be with. When they were ready to leave, Antonio turned serious again and said:

'Give me a few days and I will get you what you need.'

25

Da Costa was late arriving at the bar, blaming the traffic. The English pair already had glasses of cold Super Bock. Da Costa ordered the same. They had the list of the restaurants and bars visited at lunchtime, so they could leave them for now.

They would concentrate on those which opened only in the evenings and combine pleasure with business at one of them. They would start in the picturesque zone. But some restaurants were only just opening up, so it was possible that crucial staff might not yet be on duty.

'Maybe it will be a waste of time. But let us see. We can but try. Anyway, we can find a good place for dinner,' da Costa said.

They decided to walk along Rua del Castelo Picau, back down Rua da Reguiera into Rua de Sao Miguel and back up Rua de Sao Pedro. That would take in six restaurants which had not been open earlier. However attractive the area of narrow streets was it, was a bit of an ordeal and Tremaine found that her ankle tweaked a bit.

She wasn't going to mention it, what was the point when they were obviously going to do what they were going to do anyway. She did though ask them to walk more slowly.

They had no luck at the first four restaurants but found that at the fifth, Lautranco, they struck lucky. The chef-proprietor did recognise the four men from the photos. He remembered that there was also a fifth man who was bigger than the others and noticeably balding. One of them had a curious tick, a jerking of the head.

He remembered that they were talking in English mostly about football, money and about places where they might meet next. They had ordered the more touristy dishes and didn't spend long over their dinner. Three of them were going on to a Fado bar and the other two were going back to their hotel.

He didn't know which hotel. But he got the impression that the two going back to their hotel were a couple. They had said good night to the others.

'Take care. See you next time in a month or so.' They had said.

They thanked the Patron for giving them that useful information. They now knew that it was a group of five and that they had met in the Alfama at least twice.

They decided that they couldn't do anything more that would be useful before morning, so they decided to have dinner there at Lautranco. Da Costa hadn't been to the restaurant before but he knew it had a good reputation for traditional Portuguese dishes.

He asked the others if they should just ask the Patron to bring them a selection of the specialities of the house. They all agreed and the Patron enthusiastically proposed to offer them what Redwood would have called a Tasting Menu in England. It was a generous tasting, more than they would get in England and more than they could quite manage.

Pasteis de Bacalhau (salt cod pastries), Porco a alentejana (pork belly & clams) and Frango a piri-piri, a chicken dish from the former African colonies among the dishes. The desert of Aroz doce was a rich creamy rice pudding the like of which the English detectives had never tasted.

They had ordered relatively inexpensive wines that da Costa had said were often better than some of the well know marques. He was right they were very good. At the end of their dinner, the Patron brought them Brandy and bicas, on the house.

It was 11:30 by the time they finished. Da Costa said would go home and would walk back to his car.

Presumably parked in a NO PARKING place, Redwood thought. Remarkable how the police could always find them and evidently thought they were parking spots reserved, by right, just for them.

Redwood and Tremaine were just a few hundred yards from the Castelo and walked back to the hotel. He helped her up the steps to the Castello. When they reached their rooms, Redwood said again how much he had enjoyed the evening, took her hands and kissed her cheek before they went singly inside.

Alone in her room, Julia Tremaine considered what was happening. She knew that she did enjoy Redwood's company, his seriousness, his solicitousness and indeed his good looks. She liked him and liked being seen with him. She really did like it. She didn't know whether she should make an encouraging move.

Sam Redwood had made it fairly clear that he enjoyed her company and being with an attractive younger woman. He was no cradle snatcher though; he knew that Julia was thirty two from the records that had been sent through to him. He assumed from their conversation a couple of evenings earlier that she had had a few partners and that none had lasted.

He was well aware of the inadvisability of socialising with a fellow officer especially a more junior female officer but somehow here in Lisbon, it seemed a little less important. Anyway, he wasn't compromising her ability to work nor his own. They were a hundred percent focussed on the investigation; yes, they were.

26

In the PJ on the following morning, they thought it was time to explore the possible connections between the couriers and the banks. It had to be done carefully. As they had realised earlier if the bankers discovered they were being investigated, the shutters would come down.

Gloria organised the DCs to find out what they could about the three Lisbon banks. They would have to make discrete enquiries at the Registro Comercial and the Departmento das Financas and it would be essential for them to talk only with people they knew they could trust not to alert the banks.

They asked colleagues in the Rijkspolitie and the Bundespolizei to make similar enquiries into the BWD Bank and Deutsche Bank Bremen. The Dutch and German police were asked to try to find out about any cash withdrawals that just could be suspicious or not fully accounted for.

Anything at all out of the normal activity. They would know to do that ultra-discretely and would make their own approaches to their Public Prosecutor's offices if they thought it necessary.

The Portuguese newspapers, especially the Tabloids, had always had a fascination with the lives of the super-rich. Photos of members of the old banking families frequently appeared with lurid reports of affairs, divorces, sexual malpractices and paedophile rings along with conjectures that some of them belonged to closed circle associations.

Often, there were more serious reports covering their Right Wing political connections. Tomas Lopes da Silva got a lot of coverage with two papers printing as much as they dared about suspicions that he was organising funds for extremist groups. He had never been shy of saying that he profoundly lamented the passing of the old order and how futile and wrong the new Socialism was.

The da Silva's lived in one of the ornate palaces in Sintra. A huge, ugly and vulgar pile perched towards the top of a hill surrounded by its gardens. It stuck out two fingers to the rest of the world. Sintra had always been ultra-exclusive and the comically ornate palaces had been built by the super-rich. It was a sealed colony, virtually a Lisbon suburb, inhabited by millionaires.

Gloria Esteban had a close friend in the police there. She asked her to find out what she could about da Silva's activities, to somehow get "inside" the set-up.

'Would you try to find out the workings? What happens regularly, what happens occasionally? Any happenings out of the norm. That sort of thing. But for God's sake, be careful and don't arouse any suspicions. If you think you have been rumbled, back off straight away.'

Sargento Carla Fernandez jumped at the idea. It would be much more interesting than dealing with pick pockets and booking the drunks and tarts into the cooler for the night. She knew it would be difficult; there was a virtually impregnable wall around the da Silva's.

But someone might be prepared to spill the beans, someone who had fallen out with them perhaps. They can't have been universally liked-the super-rich rarely were. Someone must resent their haughty overbearing presence and assumed superiority.

She thought a good approach initially would be to follow the trail of the servants. She went first to the laundry in town. The workers there would have had contact with da Silva's servants. No, nothing exceptional. She went to the dairy, the butchers, the olive oil factors, the grocers; nothing out of the ordinary at all. She went to the farmacia, to the tabacaria and the newsagent, nothing unusual, nothing helpful.

She went next to the two garages. Nothing at the first but at the second, she learned that a chauffeur had been dismissed recently. For a bit of baksheesh, she got his name and a rough idea of where he lived. She drove to the edge of town and asked around in the recently built social housing estate. She was directed to the small house of Pedro Gonzalez.

He was still fuming about having been dismissed after many years of loyal service

'No pay-off, no pension; just thrown on the scrap heap,' he said.

'For what?' He had just been told that he had been indiscreet and that his services were no longer required. Full stop. Discarded just like that.

Carla Fernandez decided to probe further and dangled the possibility of some part-time driving for one of the police officers who had had a crippling accident.

Gonzalez took the bait and continued. He said that, when a bit drunk in the local bar, he had mentioned that he had driven locked tin boxes to various posh addresses in Lisbon. He didn't know what was in the boxes but he had described their appearance. Someone must have snitched, word had got back to da Silva and he was fired the next day.

Sgt Fernandez thanked him for talking to her, gave him fifty Euros and said she would be in touch about the driving. Once outside, she phoned Gloria and told her what she had found out. When Carla Fernandez described the boxes as detailed by the chauffeur, Gloria knew immediately that they were the Transit boxes.

Here was a link then. Tomas Lopes da Silva, the Banco Caixas and the as yet unknown receivers in Lisbon.

27

Da Costa called the investigating team together. How should they find the receivers?

'Obvious really,' Gloria said, 'ask the chauffeur where he took the boxes and work from there.'

Pedro Gonzalez didn't have a telephone. Gloria phoned Sgt Fernandez and asked her to pick up the chauffeur and take him to the station in Sintra. She and da Costa would drive over to Sintra and talk with him there.

Redwood and Tremaine couldn't contribute much to this process, so they excused themselves from the PJ to do some "informed" sightseeing. They had clocked the image of the Elevador de Santa Justa in the photo of the four men, so they decided to have a look at it for themselves. It would be a welcome change from being in the closed interior of the PJ.

They felt that some walking and a bit of sightseeing was due. They took a taxi to the centre, the Baixa, Lisbon's high class shopping area and walked through it towards the Chiado. They had a map. Julia had sensibly bought a guide to Lisbon in WH Smith Heathrow, so that she could read up a bit on her flight out.

They walked along the Rua de Santa Justa and there it was-eight storeys of filigreed iron. She read out that it was designed by a French architect, du Ponsard who had been a pupil of Gustave Eiffel. Yes, they could see the stylistic connection. They took the teak panelled elevator to the uppermost platform from where they could see the gridded layout of the Baixa below. They could see the Alfama beyond the Baixa and the Castello de Sao Jorge sitting high at the end of it.

'The castle looks best from here I think, Julia-up close you can tell that it is a reconstruction, rebuilt on the orders of Salazar in 1938 as a matter of fact.'

'Yes, it is a fantastic skyline. I'm going to look in the book to see what that large church is. Yes, it says here that it is the Santa Engracia and that Vasco de

Gama is buried there. See, Sam there is sometimes a benefit in having a guide book. But it doesn't mention that the castle is a reconstruction.'

'Well it wouldn't, would it?' Sam said, 'We are all supposed to believe it is medieval.'

Sitting in the sun at the café, they had a fresh orange and a Pasteis de Nata. The panoramic view of the city and the Tagus estuary was marvellous and they felt very pleased to have got out on their walkabout. The peace was interrupted by a phone call from Gloria who said that the ex-chauffeur had been very helpful and had agreed to show them the places where he had made the deliveries. They were on their way to have a first look at them and to note the locations exactly.

When they had finished at the café, Redwood and Tremaine walked on towards the Biarro Alto. They stopped several times to take in the views across the city below. They could see the Mostiero dos Jeronimos and the Torre Belem far down to the right.

'If we get the chance, we should go to the Mostiero Julia. I remember the monastery as being superb, entirely late Gothic and very flamboyant.'

When they reached the Largo do Chiado and the now familiar Brasiliera, they felt they had played truant for long enough. At the tram stop in the square, they looked at the routes and destinations. They could see that any one of them would take them back down to the Baixa.

They got on to the first tram to arrive. It was curiously old fashioned, basic and functional. It leaned alarmingly this way and that and they hung on for dear life as it hurtled at phenomenal speed rattling down the rails through the Chiado to the Baixa.

'As good as a fairground ride.' Redwood remarked when they had got off.

They were both left slightly breathless. From the Baixa stop, they took a taxi back to the PJ.

There, they found that Gloria and da Costa had brought the chauffeur in with them as a reward for being so helpful. They introduced him to the English, gave him a quick tour of the building, thanked him again and then sent him back to Sintra in an unmarked police car. He sat in the back of the car smiling as he waved goodbye. He had enjoyed being feted.

They had noted the addresses where Pedro Gonzalez had made the deliveries. Now, they needed to find out who lived there.

Gloria asked two of the detective constables to search the Electoral Roll for the two districts. Once it had been brought it up on the screen, they all gathered to look for the three addresses. The listings gave them the information they needed.

In the sequence in which they had travelled with the chauffeur, they first looked up the two villas in Restello. Two luxury gated villas in an area of luxury gated villas.

No. 9 Rua Paolo de Gama was listed as the home of General dos Santos.

No. 11 Rua Fernao Gomes was the home of Michael de Klerk.

Then in Santo Antonio, another exclusive area around the Botanical Gardens, they looked at 15 Rua da Alegria. It was listed as the home of Frederick von Hugel.

The whole team now needed to delve deep and find out as much as possible about these people, the receivers. They discussed how to do this and arrived at a plan.

Gloria Esteban would make enquiries at the Spanish Embassy. Dos Santos was a Spanish name, so they should know about the General. De Klerk was a Dutch name. Most Dutch people spoke English, so Redwood and Tremaine would visit the Dutch Embassy.

No-one in the team spoke German but a pair of Detective Sergeants would visit the German Embassy and hope for the best. Da Costa and the DCs would remain at the PJ to co-ordinate any information they fed back as the enquiries were made.

Gloria found the junior attaché at the Spanish Embassy to be openly helpful. He quickly brought up the Embassy's records on General dos Santos. He had left the Army eight years ago under a cloud. He had been exposed as a sympathiser of the banned extremist group ETA and had been quietly shunted into a retirement he had resented.

He had moved to Lisbon the following year. There had been nothing left for him in Spain. Since being in Lisbon, he had been in at the start of the new group Chega or Enough. This was fantastically useful information. Gloria gave the junior attaché one of her warmest smiles, thanked him and left. The smile kept the attaché going for the rest of the day.

At the Dutch Embassy much to their surprise, Redwood and Tremaine found that Michael de Klerk was a principal under-secretary there at the Embassy. The young clerk taking their enquiry could tell them little more except that de Klerk was pretty senior and had been in post for six years.

He couldn't say anything further. They thanked him all the same. They hadn't learned much but they had learned that de Klerk was in a position of influence. Maybe he was the doorkeeper or the enabler?

The two detectives visiting the German Embassy had more of a struggle. They had assumed that their reasonably fluent English would get them the information they needed. The desk clerk didn't fully understand what they were after so they asked to speak with a staff member who was fluent in Portuguese.

Telephone calls were made and five minutes later, a severe looking woman probably in her early '50s, came down the stairs to greet them. They explained what they wanted to find out. The woman disappeared back into the offices and came out five minutes later with part of a register of Germans known to be living in Lisbon.

Von Hugel was a businessman with interests in the arms trade who had companies registered in tax havens internationally. He had lived in Lisbon for seven years. They thanked her for the information, she gave them a thin smile and went back upstairs.

28

Three days after they had had lunch at Peniche, Antonio rang Gloria to say he had something for her.

'Can we meet at cafe Arte - 12:00? It will be busy, so we can be lost in the crowd.'

A bit before 12:00, Gloria got to the smart cafe in the Baixa and found a table. He arrived on time and kissed her on the cheek. They were to look like an ordinary couple. He passed a packet over, which she put into her bag. They drank their coffees and chatted as if they were untroubled by events.

Just an ordinary day for ordinary people. They looked like a perfect couple on a day out. But what they were doing was so serious that they couldn't find a way to sustain their informal chat. It was as if the impending action had frozen them.

Glancing at his watch, he said:

'I should get back to the bank.'

'Look, I really do enjoy being with you Gloria and I hope we can meet again. And soon. I wish you were free, I really do.'

He got up, took her hand, kissed her again and walked away.

'Well, maybe I will make myself free,' Gloria thought, 'yes, I might well do that. Yes, I think so. Time for some sort of change anyway.'

She took a taxi back to the PJ. In the case room, she beckoned to da Costa and opened the packet. There were thirty or more pages detailing bank transactions. They studied them page after page but whatever story they told remained a mystery to them.

The documents would have to have to be analysed by someone who could make better sense of them than they could. They considered who to ask. Then they both realised that they had someone on the spot who could have a first look.

They thought that Jaime Delfonso, the Finance officer, was honest and straight and that they could trust him to have a look at the documents. Da Costa took the packet and went upstairs to Delfonso's office.

Whilst he was upstairs, Gloria had a phone call from Carla Fernandez who could hardly speak; she was extremely distressed and was trying to hold back tears.

'Pedro Gonzalez has been killed—killed at his home. He was shot in the head. It is just so awful, Gloria and to think we must have caused it. Someone must have noticed our interest in him and reported back to the da Silva's.

He must have been got at by someone working for them, who else would have done it? SOC officers are there now and I must go over to see if they find anything that can point us to his killer. It is just so awful, awful.'

Gloria relayed all this to the team and they were all visibly shocked. The room went quiet and remained so for quite a while.

'We can't brood on this,' Da Costa said 'we should have been more careful and we shouldn't have brought him back here. We were just being friendly and grateful but someone must have noticed and that has led to this dreadful crime. I am in charge here and it is me who should have made a better decision.

The blame stops with me. You are not responsible. We have to carry on and we will find who killed him, it is the only way we can exonerate ourselves and give the man some justice. Focus your minds on that.'

At the end of the afternoon, Delfonso asked to talk to da Costa. He suggested that they should meet in the lobby and go for a coffee together. He would bring the packet. They selected Cafe Minerva just around the corner. It was busy but still had some free tables outside. Once they had ordered their drinks, Delfonso said.

'Luis, this looks like it could be dynamite. It is beyond my expertise but I think it looks very fishy. I can't see where the cash originates or its end destinations. It certainly isn't a record of orthodox banking. If it is a trail, there are plenty of in-built diversions. It is your call, of course but I would take it to the Public Prosecutor.'

Da Costa did just that. Having made an appointment for a mid-afternoon meeting with the Assistant Deputy Prosecutor, he went over with the packet. The youngish Prosecutor opened the packet and leafed through the pages. Da Costa assumed that he was one of the "high-fliers" newly appointed after a clear out of some of the dead wood who were retired-on full pensions, of course.

Unlike some of the previous holders of his office, this man didn't look as if he could be easily bought. He read through the pages studiously.

'I'm not certain but this looks to be a clever attempt at disguise and concealment. It will have to be thoroughly scrutinised. I will get my senior finance officer to examine it in detail but it looks to me to be some sort of concocted log of cash withdrawals and payments. It is certainly out of the ordinary as I can't see where the money goes. Thank you for bringing it to me.

We will be rigorous in our examination and if it turns out to be what I think it is, we will call in the Fraud squad. It may all take a while but be assured, I will keep you informed.'

He thanked da Costa again, they shook hands and the policeman walked back to the PJ. He had to trust someone. He just hoped that the prosecutor was as honest as he appeared to be.

29

Carla Fernandez phoned Gloria again and said that SOC officers had found nothing at Pedro Gonzalez's house, nothing at all. The whole place was clean. They had no useful evidence, there were no clues. They had said that it pointed to the killing having been a professional hit.

'It is really horrendous, Gloria. Whoever did it may not be found. Terrible, it is terrible, I feel so guilty.'

'It wasn't your fault Carla, if it was anybody's fault, it was ours. We feel really bad about it here too. We wish we had done things differently. But keep making enquiries Carla, someone walking home or walking their dog might have seen a caller at the house, someone might have heard a shot. We must do our utmost to find the killer. Nothing less would do justice to the poor man.'

The team still had to find out what happened to the cash received by the three men. They would need warrants to search the houses and question the occupants. Da Costa rang the public prosecutor's office to ask for three Mandado de Buscas-the warrants required for them to search the houses and to question any suspects.

The prosecutor, a woman this time, refused to issue them. She told him that it would be explosive - all three people were high profile citizens in the public eye. She was immovable. Da Costa wondered if she trying to shut down the investigation. Was she in the pay of the bankers? This was frustrating. He would have to bypass her.

He phoned his Commandente-General and asked to talk with him. The Commandente had been kept informed on the progress of da Costa's investigations and agreed to see him straightaway. He was brought fully up–to-date and da Costa explained why they needed the search warrants.

The plain argument was that the extremist movements were banned in the four countries and that funding them and funding terrorism in any form was against international law. They were looking at high profile criminal activity and it was their duty to close it down by every means possible.

The Commandente nodded his agreement but said he would have to seek the sanction of higher authority. He told da Costa that he would speak to the Minister of the Interior as a matter of urgency and would inform him of the outcome. He hoped to have instructions for da Costa by the end of the afternoon.

When da Costa had left his office, the Commandente telephoned the Interior Minister on the secure line. The Minister immediately saw the case as a political hot potato with potentially disastrous spin-off. The governing party was already mired by a series of scandals and this would just dump them further into a growing mess. He said he would need to discuss the situation with his own advisors.

During the course of that discussion, they accepted that the searches would have to go ahead in line with Portugal's obligations in International Law and European Union agreements. They could see that they had no other option. But the investigations into the three suspects would have to be conducted as surreptitiously as possible.

The whole operation would have to be conducted with the utmost discretion to avoid any publicity. There would be no press releases or statements of any kind. Any questioning of the principals would have to be carried out behind the closed doors of the PJ and only the fewest possible number of officers were to be involved on a need-to-know basis.

Da Costa got the call from the Commandente.

'The Mandado de Buscas are ready for collection at the Prosecutor's office. The Interior Minister's instructions are set out in an accompanying note. These must be studied carefully and obeyed in full. It must all go smoothly. We can't afford mistakes. Is that understood Luis?'

Da Costa was now faced with the problem of putting the searches into action. It was a real dilemma; he couldn't afford for it to go wrong in any way. He discussed with Redwood possible ways of going about it. They agreed that the approaches or raids should be made early in the morning when there would be few people about—the fewest number of people to witness what was going on.

Police raids were not usual happenings in those affluent districts. The raids were to be made by the minimum number of officers with the minimum amount of show. It would all have to be as inconspicuous as possible.

At 4:00 a.m. an unmarked car drew up at each of the three villas with just one detective and two police officers in each car. The officers would be armed as usual in these situations. Da Costa, Sgt Esteban and an Inspector were to lead. Gloria was wearing her standard issue Gen5 Glock with the holster tight against her right thigh.

By 4:30, the three protesting suspects were led out to the police cars. The detectives with one armed officer escorted each of them to a car; the second officer stayed behind at each house to ensure that documents or any other evidence would not be tampered with or removed altogether.

At 7:00 in the morning, teams of four arrived at each of the houses to make detailed searches.

There wasn't much of a paper trail in any of the houses. There wouldn't be. These men were careful. They would have ensured that their tracks had been covered. No cash hoards were found and if they had been, they expected that the serial numbers of the notes would have been random in order to make them untraceable. These were not stupid men. They and their advisors would know every trick in the book.

Evidence would have to come from outside. The Prosecutor's office would have to come up with the goods if prosecutions were to succeed.

30

At the PJ, General dos Santos, Michael de Klerk and Frederik von Hugel were put into separate interview rooms.

The police officers didn't have to exert much pressure during their questioning, they had just to hint at it. It was well known that they could be brutal. The men were interviewed solidly for two days by officers working in shifts. They became tired and the more tired they became, the more co-operative they became.

They already knew a lot about General dos Santos. The Spanish police with the co-operation of the Army had provided a dossier of known contacts between the General and ETA. He had been involved in the planning of ETA bombings and other atrocities against the civilian population.

He had organised for a supply of arms and explosives to be siphoned-off from Army depots and delivered to ETA intermediaries. They had already found his connection to Chega or Enough - the newly formed Rightest group in Portugal to which he was now channelling funds. He had continuously meddled to promote unrest both in Spain and Portugal.

He told his inquisitors that he didn't know anyone else involved in funding terrorism and that he dealt with da Silva and him alone. He knew of no network. He had no more useful information to offer. He was proud to have done what he had done. There was no contrition; he still believed he was in the right.

His lawyers pleaded dementia and ill health and that dos Santos could not be held responsible for his actions.

Von Hugel's activities were known to Interpol. Currently, he was supplying arms to Assad in Syria and Aketo in Angola. Wherever there was unrest and civil war, von Hugel was trafficking arms to the warring groups and often to both sides simultaneously. The arms trafficking deals made by von Hugel through his shadow companies were well documented and it was suspected that there were many more instances that hadn't yet come to light.

The man was an out and out unprincipled profiteer. He was buying the armaments with the funds from da Silva and making a profit on those transactions as well as taking a hefty cut. He didn't deny the activities; he refused to say anything. There was no point in doing so. He would rely on his lawyers.

Michael de Klerk turned out to be just a maverick using his position in the Embassy for personal gain. He was a facilitator, he made high level introductions and smoothed the way for rogue governments and their mercenaries to get hold of funds. He was arrogant and disdainful.

He knew he had a fortune stashed away in numbered bank accounts, which he would tap once his lawyers had persuaded the Portuguese courts to release him. He had no reason to hold back information the police wanted. He told them that he thought there were possibly four middle men like him who received cash through da Silva's operation.

He didn't know who they were. Da Silva kept everything close to his chest. He thought though that there were four or five groups operating in Europe who were receiving funds through Banca Caixas. His own role was to lubricate existing contacts and open doors to new ones.

He had concentrated on the Balkans and Libya to ensure that the funds went to the emerging Fascist groups. He took his substantial cut and assumed that the others did as well. He had a symbiotic relationship with da Silva's organisation. It had worked well for him.

The trials were held in camera to avoid press coverage and any public knowledge of a distasteful episode in Portuguese affairs. The Interior Minister wanted at all costs to avoid any fuelling of the inter-factional tensions that were troubling the country.

General da Costa was found guilty and sentenced to ten years in detention. Because of his age and frail health, he was sent to a provincial open prison. He would die there three years later.

Von Kugel was found guilty of violating international laws and trade restrictions. He was sentenced to ten years in prison. He would be in Lisbon's Central Prison - a grim building nearly a hundred and forty years old which was overcrowded and suffocatingly hot. His lawyers would regularly appeal for a reduction in sentence and for more lenient conditions. They would continue to do this for years.

Michael de Klerk was found guilty of receiving illegal funds and holding them for his own use. Fraud and money crime were always regarded as lesser offences, especially in Iberia where there was a general reluctance to declare sources of income or pay tax of any kind.

His well-paid lawyers were able to get him released on parole. He was cashiered from the embassy and retired to Switzerland in well-funded disgrace.

31

The case was now to be closed. The Minister of the Interior was insistent that he didn't want any further enquiries to be made. The PJ had managed to keep the operation under wraps and he wanted it to stay that way. General dos Santos and von Hugel were in jail, de Klerk had been disgraced and was out of action.

The donor banks had been hit and had closed all suspect accounts. The couriers were dead. Da Costa and his team would keep continue to keep watch on da Silva in case any attempt to fund illegal Right wing groups appeared again. The activities of Chega in Portugal would give them plenty to be concerned about in the immediate future.

Banca Caixas was being prosecuted for money laundering and other illegal covert transactions. The Public Prosecutor had been true to his word and had compiled a strong case detailing the illegal activities of the bank.

But the bank's highly paid lawyers would keep the case rumbling through the courts for years and da Silva would remain remote and protected. It was never going to be any other way. At least the flow of funds to the terrorist groups had been stopped, for the present.

As soon as he had realised Banca Caixas was being investigated, Lopes de Silva had alerted his counterparts in BWD Bank and Deutsch Bank Bremen. They had pulled down the shutters and halted their own operations.

All four of the couriers were dead but the killer had not been found and that was not satisfactory. At the PJ, the favoured theory was that the men had come to know too much and had become surplus to requirements. They had then been liquidated by the organisation.

'Yes, just like in The Godfather,' Gloria assured everyone 'that is how it must have been. Mafia style.'

Given the orders of the Interior Minister, they had to be reconciled to this theory.

It was time for Redwood and Tremaine to go home. They had a last all-team dinner at Gulios. Luis da Costa said he would definitely look Sam up the next time he was in London and Sam said he would certainly ask for his help at the

Met if the situation arose. Gloria said she would keep Julia posted on her love life.

They all agreed that they had liked working with each other. The parting was very much Portuguese style with much hugging and kissing. They all said their goodbyes for now and the English went back to their hotel. Redwood settled their bills.

When she looked at him questioningly, he said he would reclaim the costs once back at the Met. They walked up to their rooms. Redwood lightly touched her cheek and said good night. They arranged to meet for breakfast at 7:30.

They took a taxi to Portela airport and a BA morning flight back to Heathrow. From there, they took a taxi to the Met. Redwood signed in briefly and picked up the Mercedes from his parking slot.

He had insisted on driving her back down to Somerset. He would also collect a few clothes and fishing gear from his sister's house. It would be no bother at all.

The A303 was relatively quiet and even the slow-down at Stonehenge was freer than usual. Julia felt increasingly tense as the journey went on. They had been working closely together for more than three weeks, they had wined and dined together and had enjoyed each other's company. She regarded the oncoming parting with something much more than regret.

They got off the 303 at the Sparkford roundabout and took the B road towards Sandford Magna. Redwood parked outside Julia's cottage. They went inside. They stood looking at each other for a minute, then smiled and headed upstairs with intent.

Julia was promoted to Inspector in recognition of her work with Redwood and the Lisbon team. Detective Inspector Tremaine! It didn't sound bad. She had worked hard to get to this level.

From his Chelsea Mews house, Redwood telephoned her most evenings. They had both realised that what they had was not just a fling. Neither wanted to pressurise the other but they wanted to find a way forward. He had made two weekend visits to Julia and she had spent a weekend in London with Sam. More and more, they valued their time together.

Two months after they had returned from Portugal, he called to say that there was an opening for a D.I. in his section at the Met, would she consider it? She did consider it, she considered it for two days. She would miss her cottage and garden, miss her friends around the village and her colleagues in Yeoford. But the Met! It would be a really good career move and she would be working with Sam again.

Outside work, they were frequently seen together. They would go to the theatre, concerts and, new to Julia, the opera. New to Redwood, carefully selected gigs. Nothing outrageous mind. Each was educating and drawing out the other.

They would be seen together in restaurants and at some official functions, once at Wimbledon and once even at Lords.

But they chose to keep some information private. It was a long time before colleagues could be certain that they were living together.

Epilogue

Jacob Drexler, a big quiet Dutchman of Jewish descent, had met the other four casually at a bar in Lisbon after a football match. The bar had been busy; he was looking for somewhere to sit and asked if he could use the end of their table.

The four were quite well oiled and well-disposed to everyone at large, everything was just fine. Nothing was too much trouble. They readily agreed. Yes, join us. He told them it was his first visit to Lisbon and that he only went to the match by chance.

He had thought it was a good opportunity to see what it was all about. He enjoyed the game but said he would have enjoyed it more if he had understood the tactics and the rules. They thought that was hilarious, not knowing about football, incredible, absolutely incredible. Where had he been all his life?

The four men became vociferous and boastful, loudly pontificating about what they knew about Lisbon; where to go, what to do, where to hear the best Fado, where to hire girls or boys and then onto which football team was the best, who the greatest players were and how much their clubs had paid for them. They were on an unstoppable run.

As they drank more, they let their guards down. Santa Cruz and Casals began to boast about their political leanings, their ultra-Right connections and their PIDE and Falangist backgrounds. During the Salazar years, they had hunted down political opponents and partisans in the mountains north of Lisbon. They had many successes back then; when they caught the rebels, they had executed them. Sometimes, they would make whole village communities pay as a lesson to all.

Now they were on a mission to purify, a crusade to rid their countries of unacceptable immigrants. Santa Cruz and Casals were both active in the new group Chega, which was fermenting disquiet in Portugal. Promoting white supremacy and attacking immigrant communities.

They needed more members, he should join Chega! No, de Vries said, he should work to keep the whites in charge of his own country The Netherlands;

the blacks and coloureds should be forcibly repatriated, sent back to the old colonies, sent back up the trees, that is what PVV would do.

He should join PVV. The Jews should be thrown out too, Otto Kummel chipped in; we thought we had sorted out that problem once and for all in the Fuhrer's time. They worked themselves up into a frenzy of hate.

In 1967, Drexler's father Joost and his uncles Markus and Kees had been murdered by PIDE in a mass reprisal on a mountain village in which they had been having a break in a day's walking. A village cafe had been bombed out. They had been having lunch there and had been killed outright.

Eight others including twin girls of nine had been killed by the huge blast and several more had been injured. Santa Cruz and Casals had boasted about it when drunkenly detailing their past activities in the bar.

There and then in that bar in Lisbon, Drexler decided to keep close to the four, to learn what he needed to know about them and their pasts. He would encourage them to tell more about their despicable activities. He resolved there and then to hunt them down and to kill them one by one. He would be the avenging angel. Not just for his father and uncles but for all the people they had vilely damaged or killed.

His method would be informed by some of the best detective books. He enjoyed the way the best Crime Fiction was painstakingly researched and from the books, he learnt what he needed to know. When he felt he was ready, he embarked on a deadly game to settle scores.

He had kept in frequent touch with the four men, they met at football matches. He still wasn't interested in football but they were. It was a good way to meet. They would always go to bars after the matches. They told jokes which were foul in their own languages and were even worse transposed into English. He tolerated their poisonous views and crude language. Sometimes, de Vries and he would talk together in Dutch but mostly they all talked in English.

The four really liked the Dutchman; the "other" Dutchman as they called him who always laughed at their jokes and was generous in buying drinks. He was regarded as one of them. They gave him notes of their addresses and mobile numbers.

'Anytime you are in Lisbon,' 'The Hague,' 'Dortmund,' they each said, 'give me a call and we will go out on the town.'

He did visit them, one by one and to deadly effect. It took a while but the job was done.

He had learned from the other three that Casals had disappeared. Drexler remembered him boasting about his time in PIDE. How he had been in charge of the mountainous region of the Serra. How his cadre had tracked down partisan fighters and executed them. Summary justice, no need for trials he had said.

The Serra was not densely populated and after three weeks, Drexler found Casal's refuge near Olerios in the Serra de Alvelos. As he stepped out for his evening airing, Drexler whacked him, dragged the body back inside and tied him to a chair. When Casals came round, he didn't realise at once what had happened. Why was the "other" Dutchman here? Why was he strapped to a chair?

Drexler wanted information on the others, now Santa Cruz had also disappeared. Applying some techniques Casals would have recognised from his PIDE days, Drexler got what he needed.

He learned that Santa Cruz had fled to England and had told Casals that he was going to Somerset.

Casals didn't know where Hummel was. He didn't know where de Vries was either.

If they weren't at their apartments, he had no idea where they could be. Drexler applied a bit more pressure but clearly Casals didn't know any more. Most cruel men aren't brave and Casals certainly wasn't. He had started blubbing and his face had become a mess of tears, spittle and snot.

Drexler didn't think he would get a lot more out of the sweating Spaniard who had also pissed himself. He didn't like the stink, so he finished Casals off with the garrotte. Then, he cut him loose from the chair and put the chair back where it had been. He threw the restraining rope in the fire, scuffed over the dirt floor and walked out.

It took nearly three months to find Santa Cruz in Somerset. He had all the local maps from his previous holiday visits. He started at the Dorset border in Chard then eastwards across to Crekerne, Yeovil, Sherborne and Shaftsbury then up to Mere on the Wiltshire border and back across to Wincanton, Shepton and Cary.

He picked out isolated houses and small settlements, which he spied on one by one. It was a painstaking process but he was methodical. He would call at village stores and show a photograph of Santa Cruz saying that he was a cousin who had gone missing. The family was concerned about him, had they seen him? He had noted which shops made deliveries and he concentrated on them.

Yes, there had been luck involved. He had followed vans delivering foods from the small towns and villages and success at last came with a Greengrocer's delivery in Yurleigh. Charlie's Fresh and Fruity had made a delivery to a small cottage. When the door was opened, he could see that it was Santa Cruz who took in the box of fruit and vegetables.

He waited until it was fully dark and then knocked at the door. Santa Cruz was surprised to see him with a blackjack in his hand. He didn't need anything from Santa Cruz except his mobile phone so he took that, waited until the man was conscious again, then killed him nice and slowly with the garrotte.

Santa Cruz had always been a dapper dresser and more concerned about his appearance than the others. Drexler thought he would give him an appropriate send off, so he dragged the body down to the pond and shoved it in. You won't look so smart in the morning now, will you Senhor Santa Cruz?

De Vries had never taken flight; he hadn't thought anything was the matter. Yes, Hummel seemed to have left Dortmund but so what? Maybe he had had enough? He had continued working on his scaffolding contracts and had continued with his established routines. He had continued with his PVV activities of beating up hapless youths.

Drexler knew where he lived, the address was on Santa Cruz's mobile phone and it was the same as the one he had been given. He started to watch him closely. He knew then the rambling park where he went jogging and the time he went there every morning. It was easy. Drexler hid in bushes next to the cinder path and, as de Vries came by, whacked him and carried on whacking him.

Thinking everything had calmed down, Hummel had returned to his apartment in Dortmund. He had been surprised when Drexler had rung the bell.

'Aaah Jacob, good, good; it has been too long since we had a night out together, excellent, come on up.'

Having killed all four, he resumed his life in Delft as a writer and lecturer on medieval history. He suffered no sense of guilt, the people he had killed had needed to be removed from the face of the earth.

Two had been vicious murderers and the other two were extremist thugs, whose mission it had been to make life total hell for the socially disadvantaged and Islamic immigrants in particular. All four had to be disposed of. The world was definitely a better place without them.

Drexler had been a life-long Anglophile and spoke English "like a native". He had taken regular holidays in the U.K.; he liked the South West in particular and had spent time in Somerset, Devon and Dorset. He had visited many famous places. He knew his way around. He liked the country with its gently rolling hills and he liked the people. They were like the Dutch in so many ways he thought, very easy to get on with.

He had decided to start research on another book. It would be on the Tudor palaces, particularly the vanished Nonsuch Palace. He would look at the Elizabethan Prodigy houses: Hardwick, Wardour, Longleat and Montacute.

He would study the drawings and letters of the architects: Robert Smythson and the gentlemen amateurs. He would take his own photographs - he was good at that.

He would need somewhere quiet to rent for a year. He selected Somerset, the county he knew best from his time researching a previous book on Arthur and Camelot.

He knew what he was looking for but to avoid suspicion, he went to letting agents in several towns. He went to the letting agents in Sherborne and told staff at Cot-lets what he would like. They had a number of rural cottages for let. He pretended to be openly interested and they showed him details of several.

They showed him a cottage in the small village of Yurleigh.

'A pretty quiet village, I know where it is. I would like to look at this one.'

It wasn't let and hadn't been since an unfortunate occurrence. They give him the keys, so that he could look around on his own. He drove over, parked outside, walked up the path, turned the key and entered. It looked just the same as it had done before, perfectly suitable. Yes, this will do nicely.